Livvy imagined how wonderful a knight of old must have been in comparison to modern men....

She shook herself. She was becoming as fanciful as her daughter, whom she'd just seen talking to the suit of armor. Livvy hated to admit it, but maybe Chelsie was having difficulty separating reality from fiction.

Her daughter picked up her notebook. "I'm writing a story about a knight and a lady."

Livvy stepped closer to the suit of armor that so fascinated her and her daughter, and started polishing the beastplate. She recalled stories of chivalry and dragon slaying, kinghts wearing their lady's colors in tournaments....

"Do the sword really good, okay?" Chelsie suggested. "'Cause I'm gonna charge admission and show it off to the kids coming to the wedding."

"You can't do that," Livvy admonished.

"The knight and I are going to split the money seventy-thirty."

"Sixty-forty!" boomed out a voice from the suit of armor.

Stunned into silence, Livvy gingerly lifted the heavy visor. Inside, a pair of steel-gray eyes stared back at her.

"Lord William, m'lady. At your service."

Dear Reader,

Many of you have been watching and enjoying the Harlequin movies. The December movie, *Recipe for Revenge,* is based on a Love & Laughter novel, *Bullets Over Boise,* by one of our "finds" (i.e. a first-time author). Moreover, the author, Kristin Gabriel, has another hilarious, romantic story on sale now called *Monday Man.* What happens when a mild-mannered librarian meets a tough ex-con? He's knocked to his knees, of course! I hope you enjoy *Monday Man,* and in December don't forget to tune in to *Recipe for Revenge*!

Jenna McKnight spins a delightful tale of a hero who seems lost in time and a heroine who doesn't believe in heroes. Place this complication in a drafty English castle, add a slightly kooky grandfather and one precious daughter, stir in a dash of mischief and you have *The Wedding Knight!* If you like knights in shining armor, you'll love this book.

Enjoy some love and laughter,

Malle Vallik

Malle Vallik
Associate Senior Editor

THE WEDDING KNIGHT
Jenna McKnight

TORONTO • NEW YORK • LONDON
AMSTERDAM • PARIS • SYDNEY • HAMBURG
STOCKHOLM • ATHENS • TOKYO • MILAN • MADRID
PRAGUE • WARSAW • BUDAPEST • AUCKLAND

ISBN 0-373-44055-3

THE WEDDING KNIGHT

A funny thing happened...

What're friends for?

There I was, sitting in a slightly dusty house (maybe a bit beyond *slightly*), trying to decide which to do—clean, or write a knight-in-shining-armor romantic comedy. I doubt I have to tell you which one I chose. Fortunately, a friend called with the phone number of an exceptionally good, all-male housecleaning team. Now I ask you, what woman in her right mind would turn that down? (Okay, the dust was way beyond *slightly*.) And wouldn't you know, the big guy who now cleans my kitchen just happened to spend his formative years poking about in ancient castles and storing up all sorts of useful information.

Now that the book's written, you'll find a lot of love and laughter in these pages, but nowhere will you find the number of the all-male housecleaning service. I want to keep that magic all to myself!

—Jenna McKnight

You can write to Jenna at P.O. Box 283, Grover, MO 63040-0283. Include a SASE if you'd like a bookmark.

Books by Jenna McKnight

Prologue

*Somewhere in Europe,
five hundred years ago*

MARSH CASTLE hadn't changed in Sir William's long absence—at least not on the outside.

Shifting his hot, travel-weary body in the saddle, he relished the breeze on his face. It gave him some relief from the stifling confines of his armor while he perused his ancestral home.

Apparently Marsh Castle had fared better than he in the last six years; nary a new scar marred the stone curtain wall nor the towers, which was more than he could say for his body.

Now that he was home, it was time to lead a quiet life—take an obedient wife and produce many heirs. Time to stop fighting battles that weren't his and let the world change all it wanted.

He'd see to it that Marsh Castle did not.

He eased his mount forward, relishing the sound of his steed's hooves on the wooden drawbridge and already anticipating a long, peaceful winter in front of the fireplace in the great hall.

"Open the gate!" he bellowed toward the silent gatehouse above him.

"Who goes there?" The gatehouse, built for defense, concealed the owner of the voice inside, but not his sleepiness.

"Sir William Marsh."

"M'lord!"

"Aye, and we'll talk about your duties later, you lazy simpkin."

Rapid footsteps slapped on stone, and the voice within urgently alerted others of the unexpected arrival. Hinges creaked as the gate swung wide. With gold spurs, William urged his mount forward and entered the bailey.

A small crowd was gathering. A male servant dashed forward and took William's horse by the bridle.

"Lord William!"

So, it's true then. His father was dead. By the time the news had caught up to William, two years had passed.

"We thought you were dead, m'lord."

William dismounted and tucked his great helm in the crook of his arm. "As you can see, I'm quite well."

"Yes, m'lord. You'll be needing help. Perhaps my son would do until you've had time to acquire a squire?"

"Why are there men camped beyond the wall?"

"They are the laborers, m'lord, from Newtown and Spalding. Some even from as far as Turnbridge. Work starts on the castle today."

"Work? What work?"

"Oh, 'tis going to be grand, m'lord, the changes Lord Ed—uh, your brother's making. 'A new great hall, like none seen before,' he says. With a stronger keep, more towers on the wall—"

Changes?

"Where is my brother?"

"In your father's study, m'lord. I'll show you to him."

"I know the way, you bloody fool."

His fatigue melted away with every stride across the bailey. A woman, dragging a younger version of herself behind her, attempted to waylay him.

"A word about my daughter, m'lord?"

Out of the corner of his eye, he caught another pair rushing forth on his other side. He wanted a wife, yes, but not by sunset. And not one so blasted young.

"M'lord, if I could have a moment—"

"Silence!"

He entered the great hall—which was just fine the way he remembered it and required no changing—and, amidst the clinking and clanking of his armor, hurried up the stairs to the private study. He'd see Edward right away, hug him again, ask whether he'd married and had children. That kind of change he looked forward to.

Then he'd order the laborers away.

"Edward! Edward, I'm home!" William threw open the door to the study, where his father had been able to escape the busy household for hours—sometimes days—on end.

Edward, standing by the window, turned slowly to greet him.

A smile creased William's face, an occurrence so rare after the years away from his family that it felt strange. Even with the glare of sunlight streaming through the window, he appraised his brother with a gaze adept at sizing up a man in the blink of an eye.

"Edward, you've grown up," he said, proud to see

that his younger brother had matured into the Marsh mold of a tall, well-muscled man.

Edward's grin was tenuous. "We thought you were dead. *Someone* had to take over."

"Well, I'm home now." William stepped forward, his arms spread wide, prepared to hug his brother, but stopped short when he saw the sword in Edward's hand. "What's this? The laborers and the gateman fear no attack, yet you greet me with a weapon?"

"Father fell ill shortly after you left. For the last six years, I've run the castle and lands as *mine*."

William didn't have to have a picture drawn for him. "I see. And now you'll fight for them?"

"If I have to."

"Perhaps I should remind you that I've been fighting in one battle or another for six years?"

Edward's gaze roamed over him. "I see you have all your limbs. Have you been fighting women and children?"

William's laugh was short. As his brother took an offensive stance, William lifted his helm, prepared to don it if need be.

"You can't win, Edward. I have more experience. Why, they tell stories about my feats on the battlefield."

Edward finally grinned, undaunted by William's boast. He lunged with his sword, forcing William to draw his and deflect the first blow. "I fear your head is too big for your helm, brother. We've heard no such stories here at Marsh Castle."

William growled and slammed his helm over his head. "Then you haven't been listening." He easily deflected his brother's second thrust.

"Perhaps there's been nothing to listen to."

Edward's third thrust was meant to be incapacitating, William knew, though it was child's play for him to dodge and deflect it.

No sooner had the swords touched than the room grew fuzzy.

William took a step back and frowned. "Edward?" His brother's scowl was the last thing he saw before the room darkened.

"What black magic is this you've brought back with you, William?" Edward demanded. "Where the hell are you?"

William's equilibrium went askew. He widened his stance, but lost his balance and somersaulted through the air as lightly as if he'd been tossed out a tower window by a giant.

He could see nothing even with his eyes open, so he closed them and waited for the bone-breaking fall that was inevitable.

1

Marsh Castle, present day

"MMM-HMM." Livvy Ravenwood balanced the cordless phone between her shoulder and ear, and continued to polish dark woodwork that looked to have as much dust on it as the castle was old. About six or seven hundred years' worth, maybe more.

What *had* she gotten herself into?

"Yeah, Mom, I'm listening."

It was a tricky maneuver with the phone on her shoulder, but she also managed to reach behind her head with both hands and tug her golden ponytail in opposite directions, tightening it securely within its red satin scrunchy. She didn't necessarily *like* her hair up every day, but it was just so darned breezy on the hill outside Marsh Castle. All the time.

"I can hear you fine, Mom. You sound as if you're across town, not in Chicago. You *are* in Chicago, aren't you, Mom?"

George, her construction foreman, snickered from the antique trestle table across the room. Blueprints were spread out over the scarred top that bore testament to centuries of use, and he waited for her to get off the phone so they could discuss tearing down another wall.

Renovations were under way for the bed-and-breakfast she and her grandfather were opening soon, the wedding she'd agreed to hold at the castle was tomorrow and the end of the spit-and-polish finish she wanted on the antiques was barely in sight. To top it all off, her mother expected her undivided attention right then.

"What do you mean, 'What did I just say?'" Livvy teased. "Don't you remember, Mom?" She tugged her tunic back down over her spandex shorts as her mother went on to express grave doubts about both Livvy's attention span and mothering abilities.

Sometimes it was just easier to play the game.

"Okay, Mom. You said Chelsie called and told you a story about a knight in shining armor, and you're worried that she doesn't know the difference between real life in an ancient castle and make-believe."

She'd just put her mother's ten-minute concern into a nutshell. It didn't even matter if she was correct; it was close enough. She'd heard the transatlantic complaint before about Chelsie having "too lively an imagination for an eight-year-old."

It was a far sight better than living in Chicago and hearing things like "There's just the most darling man who walks his dog every day in the park. I'm sure if he likes dogs, he must like children, too. Eight a.m. and sixish." Better to concentrate on Chelsie's shortcomings.

"I'll talk to her, Mom. I promise."

"Listen, darling, as long as I have you on the phone…"

Uh-oh.

"…I met a wonderful woman at the beauty parlor, and she has a nephew—she swears he's just delightful—living over there somewhere…"

Livvy needed a sister. Six of them—one for every other day of the week. "Mo-ther," she warned.

"But, darling, it's just because I love you that I want you to be happy."

"I am happy, Mom. And really busy. I love you, too. Bye." She hung up before her mother could get another word in.

George grinned. "Mums are the same the world over, I suppose."

"Yeah, and I get a double dose because I'm an only child." Livvy tossed her dirty dust cloth onto the growing pile in the corner. "Now, what wall—"

Before she could finish, a loud crash echoed out from her grandfather's private study.

"Your men aren't working in there, are they, George? Grandpa'll have a fit if they are."

"No, but I'd like to talk about it again…"

She held up her finger to stall him. "It sounds like someone's moving around in there."

"Sounds like metal."

She stormed through the door. "I swear, Chelsie, you know Grandpa's rules about his study—"

Two steps into the room, she stubbed her sneakered toe on a suit of armor that lay sprawled across the floor. A little hop was all that saved her from landing on top of it. It lay faceup with the visor closed, arms and legs at angles that looked as though it had just been dumped there.

George, who had followed with a heavy step that rattled everything in his tool belt, faced her across the breastplate. "Bit of a mess."

She walked a circle around it, examining it, wondering where it had stood before it fell. "I don't remember him having one of these."

"Well, it's here, sure enough." He whipped out a steel tape and measured the armor from head to toe. His eyebrows, spattered with a trace of red paint, lifted appreciably. "Extraordinarily big one, too. Maybe he bought it for the bed-and-breakfast."

An unladylike snicker escaped. Her grandfather's share in their enterprise consisted of the castle structure itself; the financing, labor and decorating were up to her. Of the three, finance was her weak spot.

How she was going to add this heap of metal to the decor by tomorrow was beyond her. If authenticity were judged by the used-and-abused factor, this piece was as genuine as they came. The spurs even looked like real gold.

It wasn't that it wouldn't make a great conversation piece. It was that it was so rusty. Or was that tarnish?

George's tape measure disappeared somewhere in the leather tool belt, hidden among screwdrivers and wrenches. "Will you have time to scour it?"

"Oh, sure...by the turn of the century, maybe."

George immediately turned his attention to the wall on the far side of the study, running his hands over the dark paneling, rapping on it with his knuckles from time to time. Like most men, he seemed to prefer knocking walls down to cleaning them. "If we opened up this wall and enlarged the room..."

Livvy heard the gasp behind her; her grandfather, no doubt. She hadn't seen him in nearly a week—he liked his time alone—and it would be rotten luck for him to show up at the moment. She whirled around, ready to offer a quick assurance that she'd let George do no such thing.

But her grandfather wasn't there. Nor was anyone else.

Arms spread wide, George rambled on, "...and then we could open this up over here."

There it is again.

"Did you hear that?" Having difficulty placing the source of the sound, Livvy peeked out the doorway into the other room. Not a soul in sight there, either.

George rapped on the wall. "I don't know... Sounds normal for these old structures."

She nudged the tarnished suit of armor with her toe and wondered how she'd get it clean by morning. If there'd been a closet in the room, she would've hidden it in there. It wouldn't fit in any trunk she could dig up.

"We could start tearing that wall down right after the wedding's over," George concluded, still off in his own world of tear-down-and-rebuild.

Definitely a gasp. Definitely a sound her grandfather would make if he suspected anyone even *thought* of rehabbing his study. Definitely coming from down around her feet, a notion which only made her realize she'd inadvertently inhaled too many cleaning chemicals today.

"I say, are you all right?" George asked.

She smiled so he wouldn't worry about her, and tipped her head to one side to stretch cramped neck muscles. "Unless suits of armor can make noise on their own, I guess I'm just overtired."

He smiled sympathetically. "My wife always gets extra tired when she's expecting, too."

Livvy's hand landed reflexively on her stomach. She didn't even need maternity clothes yet—not as long as spandex shorts and tunics were available— and it surprised her when someone knew she was pregnant. A single mom, she'd only been in Europe for three months. She didn't know anyone who could have gossiped about her. Of course, with an eight-year-old resident blabbermouth like Chelsie, who could *not* know?

She debated on not polishing the armor, but she owed her neighbor, Leo, a pile of money. His only child, a daughter on whom he doted, was getting married in the castle tomorrow "for atmosphere." Livvy didn't have much choice about that, but if she had her way, all the guests would be walking billboards when they left after the reception.

"Guess I'd better go find some metal polish."

"You're sure you'll be all right?"

She smiled with what she hoped was reassurance. "Sure. I can just sit here on the floor by it and rub away."

Did it have to be so darned big? Though, if she were to imagine a knight in shining armor, he'd be about that size. Broad-shouldered, broad-chested, enough muscle to move all that metal around on a battlefield. *Yummy.*

Obviously her daughter came by her imagination genetically.

George shoved the desk chair up behind Livvy's knees. "You should sit down. You've been working too hard."

"What?"

He leaned down for a closer look. "You're all red in the face."

She pushed him out of her space. "Don't be silly."

His eyebrows puckered as he wisely changed the subject. "About this wall, then…"

"It's not that I think it's a bad idea, but Grandpa—"

"It'd make a grand suite."

"—won't change a thing in here. It's the only room in the entire castle he won't have changed, so it stays."

With one last, lingering look at the wall, he sighed and gave in gracefully. "Okay, you're the boss. Guess I'd best get going."

"Mmm-hmm." Livvy turned her thoughts to analyzing the best way to tackle the tarnished armor project. Chelsie craved stories about knights and ladies; maybe if Livvy came up with something imaginative, she could con the little munchkin into helping for a while.

Anything to keep away the R-rated fantasy that was fighting for her attention as she stared down at the heap of metal that used to cover the body of a rather large knight.

WILLIAM HADN'T SURVIVED six years of battles without learning some strategy. Not that he'd ever been unseated on a battlefield, of course—and he'd cut out the tongue of the first man to say so—but he'd dealt with opponents who had tried to fool him by playing dead. He lay absolutely still until George and the lady left the room, when what he really wanted to do was throw open his visor and see if the lady's beauty matched the sweetness of her voice.

But he steeled himself to remain motionless. He'd nearly given himself away when George had proposed tearing down the wall. Had Edward no shame? Would George and his camp of laborers tear down all of the Marsh ancestors' walls before Edward was through? Was the lady Edward's wife?

By the saints, I hope not!

If so, coming home and coveting his brother's wife was going to cause unanticipated difficulties, indeed. Of course, once William got up, found Edward and finished the fight over the castle, chances were good that Edward would take his wife and leave.

William had only caught a glimpse of the lady through the sights in his visor as she'd stood over him, discussing his armor as if she'd been a squire. But what he'd seen! Hair the color of a wheat field, though why it stuck off the back of her head like a horse's tail was beyond him. If that was the way fashion had gone in his six-year absence, he didn't like it much.

She had fair skin, and lips that smiled easily. He'd not been able to see lower than her shoulders, yet estimated her to be tall for a woman, and slender.

He remained still as he heard George shuffle about in the outer room. By the time the coast was clear, and William was ready to roll over and haul himself to his feet, a young girl skipped into the room and pounced on his chest.

"Cool! Grandpa's got a knight."

He sighed. Quietly. It wasn't that she was heavy. It was that she bent over and peered through the sights in his visor.

Perhaps she was naive enough that, if he continued to hold very still, she wouldn't know he was in there, in spite of her leaning so close that he could see freckles on her nose. A yellow stick was perched over her right ear, pinned between it and her blond head. Her eyes were sky blue, the same color as his mother's.

Speaking of whom, he would visit her straightaway after dealing with Edward. He'd have to apologize for fighting with his brother, of course, and probably for Edward's imminent departure.

The young girl straddled his breastplate, picked up his left arm and tested the joints.

"I'm Chelsie. I live here. Did you come for the wedding?"

Ah, maybe the lady is only Edward's future *bride.* Maybe she wouldn't leave with Edward.

"Are you a real knight?"

He'd had a daughter once. He knew the questions would be endless unless his silence convinced her there was no one in the armor.

"Have you ever been to a tournament?" she persisted.

He wanted to bellow at her to get off his chest and quit asking such foolish questions. Had he ever been to a tournament, indeed! Where else did she think he got the practice he needed for battle?

"Is that a real sword that ever hacked off anybody's head?"

It was all he could take. With a deep breath, he raised his chest beneath her, hoping to frighten her away.

Apparently she was strong of heart, as she didn't budge. His growl was equally useless.

"Well, did it?"

"No, but it cut out a little girl's tongue once for not knowing her place."

Her petite lips broke into a wide smile. Her eyes glittered as if she'd just discovered a treasure. "Awesome!"

He should have known better. Something about the impudent little maid should have told him.

"Then I can charge money to let the kids touch

your sword at the wedding." Her brows puckered and her lips pursed in thought. "I'll split it seventy/thirty with you if you tell them the story about cutting out the little girl's tongue."

What curse is this Edward has brought on me?

He'd used magic to cast him through a black void and then he'd sent this child to annoy him to death. She didn't even have the decency to be frightened when he grasped her around the waist and lifted her off of him. Nor when he got to his feet and towered over her. She just stood there staring up at him with a mercenary gleam in her big blue eyes.

She slid the stick out from above her ear. "I'll draw up a contract. Grandma showed me how."

Footsteps drew near. William preferred to have the element of surprise.

"Is it a deal?" Chelsie asked.

"Silence," he ordered, concentrating on the footsteps. One set or two? The angel or Edward?

Chelsie parked her hands on her hips. "Seventy/ thirty. That means I get seventy percent and you get thirty."

He'd never been bested by anyone, much less a precocious child, but, if he stood there and continued to bargain with her, he'd lose his advantage. Quickly he backed up against the paneled wall and made to draw his sword, but it lay on the floor, several paces away. He grasped his poleax instead, hefted it in his hand until he had just the right balance.

He whispered, "You may keep half for yourself if you don't give me away."

"Nuh-uh, mister." She had one of those horsetail hair arrangements, also, and it whipped from side to side as she shook her head. "It's my great-grandpa's castle, not yours."

"Chelsie, is that you?" The inquiry floated into the room before William could argue the point.

He closed his eyes and sighed. He didn't have time to haggle. He had a fight to finish and he preferred to win.

Chelsie chewed on the end of her yellow stick and squinted up at him. "We'll go sixty/forty. That's the best I can do. Take it or leave it."

"Agreed." *And a pox on your grandmother.*

A TIN OF METAL POLISH and a rag in one hand, steel wool in the other—just in case—Livvy returned to her grandfather's study. She found Chelsie staring up at the suit of armor and, if she wasn't mistaken, *talking* to it.

Livvy hated to admit it, but maybe her mother was right. Maybe Chelsie was having difficulty separating reality from fiction. Maybe letting her follow her great-grandfather and the workers around, listening to the stories she begged them for, wasn't such a good idea. But she'd never displayed so much interest in reading and writing before; she was seldom seen without a pencil tucked above her ear and a notebook in her hand.

"There you are," Livvy said. "I was looking for you."

"It's not time for bed."

"Of course not."

"And I already had a bath."

Livvy grinned. "You mean you'd rather help me polish up this old armor?"

Chelsie picked up her notebook and put graphite to

paper. "I'd rather you tell me how to spell 'armor.' I'm doing a story about a knight and a lady."

"Who told you this one?"

"Nobody."

"*A-r-m-o-r.* Speaking of which—" she pushed against the suit and found it as solid as a stone wall "—how did you get this upright?"

Chelsie concentrated on her script as she answered, "It got up on its own." She shot a big wink in the armor's direction, adding fuel to her grandmother's argument.

Livvy stepped closer to the suit of armor, sizing it up. It was taller than she by quite a bit. George had been right—whatever knight had owned this had been a big man for the times. Probably very muscular. Very athletic.

Or maybe it wasn't the genuine article at all. Whatever the case, she made note of the worst spots that would require the most cleaning. She tried to tug it away from the wall and examine its backside, but couldn't budge it.

"You couldn't have moved this," Livvy said.

"I know."

"This ax…"

"What about it?"

"I don't remember it being in the gauntlet like that." She really had to lay off the cleaning chemicals. "Open the window, will you?"

"It's chilly outside."

"I know, but I could use some fresh air."

"Are you gonna clean it right now?" Chelsie asked as she cranked the nearest window out.

"Mmm-hmm, if I can figure out how to maneuver it away from the wall."

Careful to hold the tin as far from her nose as possible, Livvy opened it, dipped in a rag and started on the breastplate. The last time she'd come this close to touching a man's chest, she'd been in what *she'd* thought was a serious, committed relationship. Before that, she'd been married to her ex. Neither were particularly pleasant memories. She seemed destined to fall in love with men who liked to go their own way.

The harder she rubbed the breastplate, the more she imagined how wonderful a knight of old must have been in comparison to modern men. All those stories of chivalry and dragon-slaying, knights wearing their lady's colors in tournaments, and courtly love. King Arthur and Guinevere...and Lancelot.

"Do the sword really good, okay?" Chelsie suggested.

"Sure, honey," Livvy said absently, eager to continue with her fantasy.

"'Cause I'm gonna charge admission and show it off to the kids coming to the wedding."

"Chelsie," Livvy admonished, "you can't do that. The children will be guests, just like their parents."

"Uh-huh."

"No," she said firmly.

"But we're going to split it seventy/thirty!"

"Chelsie—"

"Sixty/forty!" boomed out from the suit of armor, just above Livvy's ear, stunning her into silence.

There was only one possible explanation. "George?" she queried, with enough doubt in her voice to reveal her true thoughts on the likelihood of George having donned the armor to tease her.

Tentatively she reached up. Gingerly she lifted the heavy visor. Inside, a pair of steel gray eyes stared back at her. Eyes she'd never seen before.

"Lord William, m'lady. At your service."

2

WILLIAM HAD TO GIVE the lady credit. She didn't scream. She didn't swoon. She did look, however, as if she'd like to do one or the other, but hadn't made up her mind yet which was better.

He wondered briefly if she were the child's governess, but with the same shade of golden hair and identical tiny noses, they looked too alike to be unrelated.

When he'd observed her with the laborer, she'd spoken like a noblewoman. And she smelled of the most unusual spice; surely something a governess couldn't afford.

Yet, as she'd rubbed her hand over his breastplate, he'd noticed she was built like a wet nurse. All things tallied, he hadn't a clue as to who she was or what her position in his castle was.

He really needed to find Edward. Besides Marsh Castle's ownership to settle, William had a few questions that needed answers. Such as why were these females dressed in such a fashion as to bare their legs? What manner of speech was theirs? And who was she that she took a deep breath, fisted her hands on her hips and stared him right in the eyes?

"What are you doing in my grandfather's study?"

She had the same sky blue eyes as the little girl, but her temper added a sparkle that made him forgive her impudence for speaking to him—lord of the castle—in such a familiar fashion. Heaven help her if she did it in front of others, though.

"I hired you reenactors for the wedding tomorrow," she continued, "not to prowl around here tonight scaring the willies out of me."

In all his travels, he'd developed a knack for linguistics, an ability to blend in, but he'd never heard such an accent.

"Willies?" he asked. "What word is this?"

"And that armor is a disgrace." She pushed against his breastplate in emphasis, but he stood steady. In fact, her push was little more than the strength with which he would swat a fly. "Go home and clean it."

"M'lady, I am home, and my armor has stood me well. I need to find my brother, Edward. Have you seen him?"

As she capped the polish, a smile broke across her lips, though he thought she fought it. Not only the voice of an angel, but a beatific smile as well.

"That's wonderful," she said. "Can you do that tomorrow?"

"What, m'lady?" *Stare at you until I can see you in my bed?*

"That. Act like a real knight."

"But I am a real knight, m'lady. I am Edward's older brother. If you haven't seen him, perhaps your husband would know his whereabouts?"

Her smile widened, though William could see her struggle to contain it. Her lips held a tantalizing curve, and her teeth were whiter and straighter than any he'd ever seen.

"I'm not married."

Ah, a widow. He warmed to the thought of lingering a bit longer. "Your speech is most unusual. May I inquire where you're from?"

"Illinois."

"Is that in France?"

Her laugh was light and airy. Fun and, for some reason he couldn't determine, very pleased.

"You'll do very well tomorrow, I think, if you can stay in character like that."

Her horsetail bobbed, and he wanted to touch it to see if it felt as soft as it looked.

Chelsie said, "Illinois is in the United States." He must have looked puzzled, because she added, "Of America." Which didn't help a whole hell of a lot. Nonetheless he would show his gratitude for her attempt by being lenient with them for their behavior.

He was pleased to see all the weariness had disappeared from the lady's eyes as, with a playful arch of her eyebrow, she said, "You know...discovered by Christopher Columbus...1492?"

"Ah," he said with much relief. "That explains it. I left here that same year. I've heard no news of a discovery."

Chelsie paused with her stick above her book. "You left in 1492?"

"Aye."

"No, he didn't," the lady protested. "Don't believe a word he says. Come on, Chelsie, it's time for you to pick up your room."

As the lady took Chelsie by the hand, William sidestepped and blocked the door. He lifted off his helm and tucked it in the crook of his arm. "M'lady, a knight never lies."

William didn't know why it was so important to

detain her until she knew he was an honorable man. He only knew it was.

"Chelsie, honey, he's just practicing his part for the wedding."

"He's pretty good."

William warmed at the way the lady's gaze roamed over his dark hair, the tiny scar beside his left eye, then lower, lingering on his breastplate.

"Very good."

His blood heated when her tongue flicked over her bottom lip.

"I mean… Yes, he's very good at playing his part."

His heart skipped a beat, and he inhaled deeply, only to have his lungs fill with her scent—a most unusual fragrance. It was a curse Edward had cast on him, sure enough, tumbling him through a black void, then tempting him with a sassy, exotic lady—when what he wanted was a quiet, patient wife.

She took a deep breath and squared her shoulders. "What's your name?"

"William Marsh, m'lady, lord of this castle and all the surrounding land."

"Uh-huh, whatever. Please, William, my daughter's only eight. She's not used to castles and royalty and chivalry. If you're going to swear you never lie, then at least tell her the truth about playing your part so you don't confuse her."

"But, my lady, I *have* spoken the truth."

"Okay, William—"

"Lord William," he amended.

"Fine, *Lord* William—" With a snap, her rag landed on his shoulder. "I should fire you right here and now for being in my grandfather's study, but

A—I don't want to clean your armor, and B—you're too good not to show off at the wedding tomorrow.''

She picked up his gauntleted hand and shoved the tin into it. The sparkle in her eyes was William's only clue that she wasn't as mad as she sounded.

''So get yourself cleaned up.''

She spun on the ball of her foot, grabbed the little one by the hand and left without a proper, respectful farewell. If he thought his head was spinning before, it was nothing compared to dealing with…with… Who the hell was she? And what was she doing in his castle?

HE WENT IN SEARCH of Edward. William had grown up in Marsh Castle; knew every nook and cranny. At least he'd known every nook and cranny the way they *used* to be. There were doorways where none existed before, the walls were brighter than his mother liked and many of the heavy wall hangings were missing.

And then he stumbled across a whole wing that hadn't been there when he'd left.

What the devil? No one built a whole wing in six years.

He knew his mother would have aged; she'd be more beautiful. He'd known his brother would be older; taller and broader. But the one thing he'd returned home expecting to find the same was his beloved castle.

With no other recourse—not a servant in sight anywhere—he backtracked to the private quarters and searched out the lady. He came upon her in a passageway, just as she backed out of a room and said, ''Get the stuffed animals from under the bed, too,

Chelsie." Apparently she reserved her sweetest tones for her daughter.

"M'lady…"

When she saw him, she folded her arms across her chest. "If you're going to hang around, you might as well call me Livvy and make yourself useful," she said firmly. "As long as you're here, I could use help hanging the paintings in the gallery."

He thought it was an ultimatum on her part, though he chose to ignore her brazenness until he could discover what Edward had done to him. And his castle. "Very well."

As he followed her toward the gallery, he was rewarded for his tolerance by the distraction of her garments—or lack thereof. Her top half was covered decently, he supposed. She certainly wasn't self-conscious about it.

But below her waist—well, he didn't have words to describe her clothing other than it looked small enough for her daughter to wear under her skirt. The shiny black fabric hugged Livvy's thighs as if it were a second skin. And she walked with just the slightest waddle. A fast one, too, as the distance between them threatened to grow. Very unladylike, but enticing just the same.

He was so distracted that he no longer noticed how the rooms they passed through had changed—until they reached the gallery. When he saw an extra two dozen portraits, some hanging, some on the floor propped against the wall, his jaw dropped in shock. Then snapped shut.

"How dare you!" he finally roared.

She jumped, her hand fluttering over her chest as

she laughed. "My goodness. I'm not used to someone bellowing."

"What have you done?" William paced the stone floor. He glared at each impostor's likeness as though he could scare him out of his castle.

Her face beamed with pride. "I finished painting the walls yesterday. As soon as we hang the portraits, this room is done."

He halted in front of the portraits he recognized— those of his father, mother and paternal ancestors. He ran his fingers lightly over the brush strokes which painted his wife's image, before the plague had taken her from him, leaving only this memory in a gilded frame. And there was a new Edward on the wall, more mature than when William had left home, younger than when he'd returned this morning.

He felt Livvy near his side, inhaled her exotic scent again and forgot what he'd been about to take her to task for.

"My grandfather sees to those," she said. "He's kept them in good shape, but I had to clean the rest as best I could. I don't know why he doesn't care for all of them, but..." She shrugged. "Maybe when I find the right records, I'll understand."

"Records?"

"Yeah, I came over to do my roots. I'm bound to have some second or third cousins somewhere, but I haven't been able to find *any*thing I need."

She bent at the waist and sorted through the portraits, which presented him with a rather distracting view of perfectly rounded hips.

"That's why I'm staying," she rattled on. "I grew up with no more relatives than my parents—don't get me wrong, my dad was great and my mom is, too, in her own, misguided way—but I'm not about to do that to my kids.''

''Who are all these—'' he waved his arm at the other portraits ''—people?''

She cocked one eyebrow at him as if he had no sense. ''Relatives?''

''Not mine!''

She laughed lightly. ''Well, I wouldn't think so, *Lord* William, but if you want to keep this up for tomorrow, you'll have my deepest gratitude. In the meantime, if you climb the ladder, I'll hand you one.''

He refused to hang impostors' portraits on *his* walls. It was a simple matter, really, to reach out with the speed of lightning, catch Livvy by the arm as she turned away and pin her to the wall. Child's play for a knight such as he, though he took utmost care not to bruise her tender flesh.

LIVVY WAS SURPRISED by the big, black-haired lug's speed. She'd thought a man covered in armor would be more hampered than he'd just displayed. At least that's the excuse she gave herself for staring at him. It couldn't be because of his steel gray eyes, straight nose or square jaw. It couldn't be because the tiny scar next to his left eye lent him character.

No two ways about it, the ladies of old had quite a crop to choose from if all knights were as tall and fast and pleasant to look at as this one.

''That armor doesn't protect everything, you know.''

''You must explain this—'' he glanced at the portraits, then down at her garments ''—to me. All of it.''

"If you don't let go of me, I'll explain something to you, all right." If she weren't afraid of bruising her knee on his armor, she'd have shown him already.

"If I unhand you, you'll answer my questions?"

"Hello!" she called out, hoping George or one of the workers would hear her, though it was late.

For her trouble, she got a metal gauntlet clapped over her mouth, but it didn't stop her from muttering into his hand exactly what she was thinking about how typical it was to have a whole castle full of workmen and not one gentleman in sight.

As she ran out of derogatory adjectives, he lowered his hand.

"Jeez, where's a knight when you really need one?"

"I am right in front of you, and when you need my services, I shall oblige."

"Tomorrow."

He cocked one eyebrow and glanced over his shoulder. "You anticipate danger at sunrise?"

Laughter bubbled up inside her. It was glee, really, knowing she'd inadvertently hired the hit of the party with this one.

"I 'anticipate' a wedding at eleven, reception to follow."

Firing him for insolence no longer was an option; he was far too priceless. Her skills as a hostess would be the talk of the region. Leo would be delighted with "the atmosphere." And since she'd used the castle as collateral to secure a private loan from him, price was what counted. Options raced through her mind about how to humor William.

"Look, I know you want to find your brother," she improvised. "How about I go look for him while you hang the paintings?'' She added a sweet smile, but stopped short at batting her eyelashes

''Forget them.''

She appraised the unfinished room, portraits everywhere, plus one empty frame that her grandfather never quite explained. ''Can't.''

''You'll answer my questions as we search for my brother together.''

''But then I won't get any work done.''

He looked at the paintings with disdain and glowered at the room in general. ''Good, then you won't be knocking down any more walls.''

''What's that supposed to mean?''

''You're ruining the castle.''

She looked around at all she'd accomplished. She'd scraped paint, filled cracks, painted walls, rubbed the woodwork until it glistened, cleaned huge, dark portraits of people with scowling faces.

''But it'll be a great bed-and-breakfast. Guests at Marsh Castle will actually get to sleep in the most wonderful, antique beds—''

''It's *my* castle.''

''Look, this act of yours will be perfect tomorrow, but you'd better not start believing yourself. It's my grandfather's castle.''

''It's mine, and I'll fight any man who says otherwise.''

Livvy threw up her arms. ''Okay, that's it. I give up. I have too much work to do to keep humoring you. I hope you come back tomorrow and do this wonderful knight thing you're doing, but if you're not going to help me, you have to leave.''

''I shall look for my brother.''

The last thing she needed was him accidentally running across her grandfather, who lived in his own fictional world. If William was itching for a fight, as his hand on the hilt of his sword indicated, her grandfather would be tickled to oblige. Sword versus six-shooter; she wondered which would win. What a pair.

"I know!" Chelsie squealed from the doorway. "We can have a tournament!"

Livvy frowned. "Is your room done, young lady?"

"But, Mom, this is perfect." The scurry of Chelsie's feet into the room matched her rapid speech. "He's a knight. He knows about tournaments. You need money. I'll sell the tickets. We can split the profit seventy/thirty with him." Her hand landed above her ear. "I'll draw up a contract."

Livvy pointed at William. "You, go back to camp and spiff up your armor." She pointed at Chelsie. "You, go clean your room." She pinned both of them with a glare. "And I don't want to hear another word about a tournament. I have enough work to do."

"But, Mom—"

"M'lady—"

It was hard to keep a straight face as she looked at the "innocent" expressions on theirs. They deserved Oscars. She bit her lip and shook her finger at them. "I want you both on your best behavior tomorrow."

"But, Mom—"

"Not another word. Come on, I'll walk you back to your room." She wanted to make sure Chelsie got there and actually got some work done.

She didn't see her daughter toss William a wink as they left the gallery, nor his answering nod.

3

WITHIN THE HOUR, 'twas obvious to William that the black void had truly been an evil curse set on him by his brother, Edward. How else could he explain what he saw? As great a knight as he was, undefeated in battle, protector of kings, it made him fear to close his eyes—sure that he would not wake come morning.

It had been a simple matter to find the camp of which Livvy spoke. The tightly strung tents—some round, some peaked—bore colors of claret, yellow and blue that would draw an enemy's eye in daytime as quickly as a fire would on a clear night. Yet no warriors shouted a death knell.

Nor had the knights in camp posted a guard. William walked into their midst without a single challenge issued his way. And he'd thought security had been slack *inside* Marsh Castle. Instead these knights sat on felled trees and flimsy chairs circled around a large fire—big enough to burn a prisoner at the stake, but none seemed to be forthcoming—and told stories late into the night. Briefly he closed his eyes and listened to their deep voices, their laughter, their belching. 'Twas all quite familiar.

'Twas when he used his eyes that he saw things were not as they ought to be. The tents and chairs and clothing were all unfamiliar to him. And, most frightening, these men had the power to light fire in their hands.

"Smoke?"

In front of him stood a red-haired young man, nearly as tall as he, which was unusual in itself as William towered over most men. He was holding out a small packet and seemed to be friendly. William selected one of the small, cylindrical objects offered him, but backed off when the man lit his fingertip fire and aimed to burn this new thing.

"Oh, trying to quit, are you? Yeah, me, too. Name's Tom." He glanced at his wrist, at a dial that glowed an eerie green in the dark. "By rights, I shouldn't be lighting up for another hour, but—" he grinned as if they shared a conspiracy "—the wife's not watching, you know?"

William grabbed the man's wrist, careful not to touch the glow. "What is this?"

"Say, that's quite a grip you got there." Tom tapped the green light. "Looks like the real thing, but it's a pretty good knockoff, wouldn't you say?"

"What is its purpose?"

Tom stared at him for a moment, much the same way Livvy had, with his puzzled expression soon changing to one of understanding.

"Oh, I get it." He laughed and clapped William on the arm near his shoulder. "Gads, man, get out of that armor and relax a bit. We're not on until tomorrow."

Frustrated, William resumed his stroll through the camp, listening to music, though he saw no instruments; inhaling the aroma of food that made his mouth water, though he couldn't identify it; seeing wagons that had doors and windows and wheels, but no tongue to which horses could be harnessed. It all was clearly foreign, but came from no country which he had visited.

Since he'd arrived home this very morning, everything had changed: garments, speech, food, wagons, castle walls, even—and this the most unexplainable— the countryside. No forest could creep forward so far in six years.

He sat on the end of a long log, not so close that he could be overcome, but close enough to listen. The men grew accustomed to him there and, some time later, he was handed a mug of the most delicious- smelling hot brew.

He was offered another "smoke" and handed the small, hard object which made the fingertip fire. Care- fully he observed how others made its magic work, and did likewise. Not raised to be a thief, but having learned in the last six years to live by adapting to new circumstances, he slipped it into his doublet.

The hour had grown late when he heard a trilling sound, quiet enough to have been a bird, but far too near.

"Somebody's phone's ringing" was uttered by more than one man around the embers.

"Who left their phone on the stump?"

"Hey, you, pass it over here, would you?"

William had no idea what to do, so he sipped his brew and pretended he didn't hear.

"The phone there, on the stump, hand it over, okay?"

He followed a stocky man's point and saw a small, rectangular black box. "That?"

"Yeah, man, hand it over."

He obliged.

The man lifted the box to his ear for a moment, said, "Sure, I'll find 'im. Just a minute," then set it down on the log. Close to William's hip.

He glanced around. No one seemed to be watching him; apparently these knights hadn't enough sense to be wary of strangers. He reached for the box, thought better of it, then summoned all his courage and snatched it up. He looked into the tiny holes, but could see nothing. Tentatively, ready to cast it aside if it, too, burst into flames, he put it to his own ear.

"Tommy? Are you there? I thought I told you to—"

He vaulted to his feet and cast the evil, talking thing away from him to land in the dust with a thud. God's truth, he'd heard a voice come from that tiny box. How did a knight fight an enemy so small?

LIVVY'S HEART SWELLED when she heard sunrise trumpeted in. She'd worked hard to make everything perfect for Leo's daughter's wedding and reception, and this was the day. She ignored a twinge of morning sickness, threw off her covers, pulled on the costume the reenactors had lent her and met her grandfather and Chelsie in the kitchen.

Unfortunately her grandfather, busy at the stove, was wearing his usual Wild West attire: black leather cowboy boots, a gun belt with a pearl-handled pistol on his right hip and a hat in a gray so light as to be almost white.

"Grandpa, you promised."

"Promised what?" he asked innocently.

"You know. No ten-gallon hat, no six-shooter, no spurs that jingle when you walk." It surprised her to remember that William had worn spurs. Gold ones.

Her grandfather handed her a box of crackers with a grin that belied his attempt at innocence. "Is that today?"

"You know darn well it is. Go up and change."

"I've got hours yet."

"Please," she begged.

"All in good time, Livvy girl. I don't want to scare the dickens out of Silver with those strange duds you got me wearin' today. I'll change later."

"But he's just a horse—"

He pecked her cheek on his way out the door. "I'll change later. I promise."

Livvy munched on the corner of a cracker and said to no one in particular, "What am I going to do with that man?"

Without glancing up from her notebook, Chelsie said, "Look at it this way, Mom—at least he hasn't started wearing a mask and calling me Tonto."

"I guess."

Chelsie nibbled on the eraser end of her pencil. "You think Lord William will be here early?"

"I don't know." Livvy's floor-length skirt rustled as she sat at the table beside her daughter, who'd been so eager to wear her costume that she'd have slept in it if allowed. "What are you working on?"

"The story I started last night. How do you spell 'tarnished'?"

Livvy tapped the small dictionary on the table. "That's what that's for."

"But if I don't know how to spell it, how can I look it up?"

"Take your time, you'll find it."

"I don't have much time. I need to see Lord William this morning."

"His name is William. He's not lord of anything. And what do you need to see him for?"

"Stuff."

"What kind of stuff?"

"We got a business deal."

"Chelsie, I told you that you can't charge the kids any money. Besides, every knight'll have a sword."

"But, Mom, he hacked out—"

Livvy clapped her hands over her ears. "No!"

Chelsie grinned and waited for her mom to lower her hands. "Too gruesome for your stomach, huh?"

"Hacking? Yes, that's too gruesome."

William, on the other hand, was another thing entirely. Not that he'd be around after today, nor interested in a single mom with a mortgage out the kazoo. But, if he was, she didn't want to associate him with hacking anything.

Slaying was okay, though. As in dragons. She had no problem visualizing him on a white horse, sword drawn, charging forward into a breath of flame to save her.

No problem at all.

THE FAMILIAR SCENT of wood smoke teased William's nostrils. Horses nickered and stomped. Men grumbled about the early hour, though the sun warming his face was high in the sky. For a long moment before he opened his eyes, he thought he was still on his way home to Marsh Castle and had been tormented with the worst of nightmares.

Except the part about the angelic woman with bare legs; she had tormented his sleep in a much different way. Though she wasn't dressed like a lady, she acted like one. Try as he might—and he'd tried valiantly—he hadn't been able to bed her in his dreams.

"William."

Unhampered by his discarded armor, he rolled toward the vaguely familiar voice. A wiry old man, wearing a hat big enough to water the white steed on which he sat, loomed over him. Even though his costume was unlike anything William had ever seen, he suspected the object strapped to the stranger's hip was a weapon.

William pushed himself up onto one elbow, letting the borrowed blanket slide off his shoulder. "You know my name?"

"Go back where you came from."

So, the nightmare was real.

Which meant the woman was, too. A bit of heaven to lighten his hell.

"You don't belong here. This land is mine."

Dozens of fully armored knights charged past, raising dust and drowning out any question William might have asked. When they were gone, so was the old man, and William's chance for answers, too.

Chelsie.

In a world gone crazy, the little girl hadn't been frightened of him and hadn't threatened him. *She* would answer his questions. All he'd have to do was agree to any moneymaking scheme she offered.

Trumpets blew at the castle and echoed down the hill to the camp, now nearly deserted, and William thanked his lucky stars that an enemy hadn't struck at sunrise when he'd been sound asleep. He barked at the first squire he saw to help him into his armor, then lit out for the castle on foot to find Chelsie.

Trumpets, banners blowing in the constant breeze,

carriages, a crowd of well-wishers lining the road—
all these he could identify with. The festivities appeared to be highlighted by all the pageantry of a
royal procession, which made his surroundings less
confusing than the evening before—until he took a
good look at the other knights' armor. Much of it—
coats of mail, surcoats, shields—was horribly out-of-
date. Some was fashioned like none he'd ever seen.
Same with the clothing worn by the crowd.

"Chelsie," he called out repeatedly as he strolled
through the people. As the evening before, no one
took notice of him, which was damned disconcerting
considering he owned the land on which they stood.

A woman elbowed him aside and pushed her children to the front of the throng. "Aren't you supposed
to be on horseback with the others?" She didn't even
have the good grace to add "M'lord," or curtsy out
of respect to his title.

He looked down his nose at the plump, determined
mother. "Who are you to speak to me so?"

"Ooh, kids, wait a minute!" She tugged them back
and shoved the littlest boy into William's arms, then
pulled a small, black box out of her gown. "I know
we're not supposed to do this, but—" She smiled and
shrugged, then lifted the box to her eyes. "Say
'cheese.' Hold it… Good, got it!"

She tucked it back into hiding, not giving William
a clue as to what, if anything, had just happened.
"What the devil—"

"You won't be giving me away if you see me at
the castle, will you?"

"What did you do?" He pointed at her gown, as
near as possible to the fold where the box had disappeared.

"Beg your pardon?"

"The box, woman! What is its purpose?"

She patted herself where he pointed. "Oh, you mean the camera?"

"Is it magic?"

She tittered. "Magic, indeed. You should be entertaining the guests, not a housekeeper like me."

He looked her over from head to toe. "You're not Mrs. Purdy." She'd been in residence since his youth.

"I'm Sarah."

"But what happened to Mrs. Purdy?"

"Who?" Her children tugged on her hand and yanked on her skirt. "I don't know. I've lived here since 1988, and I don't know anyone by that name. Are you sure you have it right?" she asked as her children drew her away.

William rubbed his brow, not certain of anything. Either the woman was daft with dates, or he'd misunderstood.

"You really should be mounted. There's a horse over there." As Sarah disappeared into the crowd, she indicated the old man's white steed. Tied to a high tree branch, it stood quietly beneath its strange saddle.

"Very well."

LIVVY STOOD ON THE WALL walk of Marsh Castle, oblivious to the sun on her head and the breeze flapping her skirt around her ankles. Binoculars pressed to her eyes, fingers crossed, breath held, she watched the horse-drawn wedding carriage and procession wind its way through the village, between the stone, thatched-roof cottages, and up the hill.

She prayed that all would continue to go well.

Everyone in the cheerful crowd wore medieval costume, though by no means did they all represent the same century. The reenactors had tried to explain the different times and different fashions to her, but, as with today's trends, she just let it go in one ear and out the other.

The trumpeters' notes rang loud and clear, letting her experience a long-ago era right before her eyes, an experience that gave her goose bumps. The rent-a-knights wore shiny armor from head to toe and carried white banners, rippling in the breeze, emblazoned with Leo's leonine coat of arms. Their splendid, prancing horses were draped in flowing parade silk and wore plumed headpieces.

"Look, Mommy, there's Grandpa's horse."

"Did he change?" Livvy gripped the binoculars tighter, but kept her gaze glued to the procession. If he wasn't in costume, he'd spoil the medieval effect.

"Not unless you got him some old, dirty armor."

"Old, dirty…" *Oh, no.*

"Hey, I think it's Lord William."

"On Silver?" That was a hanging offense in itself. "Where?"

She searched with the binoculars until William came into focus. His helm was tucked into the crook of his arm, and she got an all-too-enticing view of his broad shoulders and straight back. Moving with the horse as one, he certainly posed a knightly picture on a white steed.

She sharpened the focus as he turned his head, and was further rewarded with a view of his coal black hair shining in the sunlight, cool gray eyes, and a strong, masculine jaw.

"Oh, my." Guinevere would've tossed Arthur *and* Lancelot over for this guy.

"What? Let me see!"

William guided the horse quietly, expertly, as he eased his way through the crowd.

"Grandpa'll shoot him for sure."

He gained access to the road too soon for Livvy's liking, putting him between the postilion riders and the drawbridge. Instead of getting the heck out of the way, he turned Silver's head toward the procession.

"What the—?" Livvy muttered. "*I'll* shoot him if he messes this up."

"*Mo-om,* let me see."

Livvy thrust the binoculars at Chelsie. "Keep an eye out for Grandpa. If you see him, stall him."

"How?"

Appraising the scene for the quickest way to reach William, she replied offhandedly, "You'll think of something."

"I'll tell him I saw Jesse James on the other side of the castle."

"That'll do it."

Livvy raced down the narrow, winding steps, cursing her long skirt, thankful for her sneakers. As she charged out under the portcullis and across the drawbridge, she spotted William in the center of the road, blocking the path of the wedding carriage. The crowd pressed forward, barring Livvy's way, but she could hear William's every word.

"I seek the little girl," his deep voice rang out. "Is she in the carriage?"

As Livvy elbowed and shoved her way impatiently through the people, she heard Leo's reply, laced with good humor. "Just my little girl."

"Bring her forth. I wish to speak with her at once."

A chuckle ran through the crowd, and Livvy

slowed her step. William was staying in character, putting on extra entertainment for everyone. Should she interfere? Or give him a bonus?

"No," Leo answered. "Now be a good man and move aside."

Livvy heard an unfamiliar sound, a whoosh of metal, perhaps? *William's sword?* She quickly resumed her march to the front, and none too gently.

"As Lord of Marsh Castle and the land on which you drive your carriage, I demand to speak with her now—or you shall pay the consequences."

"Move!" Livvy screeched at a determined backside in her way.

She burst through the front line just in time to see all her rent-a-knights backing off. From the look on Leo's face, he was confused as to whether this was a jest or in earnest. Somehow she had to put a stop to William's shenanigans without causing a blot on the bride's wedding day.

"William."

He didn't even spare her a glance as she stepped forward. She rolled her eyes and resigned herself to playing his game.

"Okay...your lordship."

"Stand aside, m'lady." His sword brandished and ready, he urged Silver—who kept a nervous eye on what probably appeared to be a very long crop—toward Leo, a proud man who wanted the best of everything for his daughter, including a wedding she'd never forget. And, if she didn't get it, he had the means to close down Livvy's bed-and-breakfast before it ever opened.

She considered throwing herself in front of the horse and fainting like a medieval maiden.

4

IN SPITE OF THE UNUSUAL saddle, William sat comfortably on the borrowed stallion and scowled at the man who had the temerity to refuse him the right to speak to "his little girl." Was he Chelsie's father? But Livvy had said she had no husband.

'Twas a most confusing situation.

With a beard and mane of the deepest black, the upstart looked vaguely familiar, like a member of that blasted Leopold clan who had tried to capture Marsh Castle a time or two.

If Edward's black magic and evil curse could send him to this strange place, could he send others as well? Others who did not live by the code?

William raised his voice so no one would misunderstand just who was in charge here. "I will speak with the young girl now or have your head mounted atop the East Tower by sunset."

"*Lord* William!"

He meant only to glance down at Livvy, but failed miserably when he saw how beautiful she appeared this morn. Gone was the horsetail arrangement. Strange that he missed it now that her hair was contained in a slip of lace similar to what his wife used to wear, though the two women were as different as night and day. His wife never would have dared speak to him in such a manner, not even in private.

"Stand aside, m'lady."

Sparks lit her sky blue eyes, though he couldn't say whether humor rode there also. Not if her tight lips were any indication of her temper.

"Move that horse out of the road."

She was decently clad today, but when she fisted her hands on her hips, it emphasized her bosom in a manner such as he hadn't seen in far too many years. Her arms and legs were covered, yet he recalled every inch of creamy soft skin in vivid detail.

He forgot what business he'd been about.

"Get your sorry hide off my horse!"

William pivoted in the saddle and glared at the elderly man who had visited him in camp. "Hold your tongue, old man, or I'll have it cut out."

He didn't obey, but drew the small weapon from his hip. "We lynch horse thieves in these here parts."

"Grandpa, stop."

Livvy positioned herself between the two of them. If he lived to be a hundred, William would never understand a woman such as she. Was this normal in this place? The attentive crowd held hundreds of other women, none of whom acted in a similar manner.

"William, get off his horse. Now."

Glancing at Livvy again was his downfall. As soon as he took his gaze off the old man, William heard the most horrendous noise—and it seemed to come from the old man's hand. The already-nervous steed wasn't as well trained as William's own mount, refused to obey the aids and sidestepped right out from under him.

William landed in the center of the road at Livvy's feet, his armor grating into the pebbles with a loud crunch. Not as loud as the weapon, but William had heard of them and considered himself lucky that his armor hadn't been pierced.

It should have been horribly embarrassing—a veteran such as he unseated in front of a lady—except she had trim ankles and a pair of the daintiest feet he'd ever seen, encased in little white slippers with ties.

She bent over him. "A little out of practice, huh?"

LIVVY ALMOST ASKED if he was okay, but one look at the twinkle in his eyes and she didn't dare. She'd heard armor was heavy. Maybe too heavy for him to get up and out of the way of the wedding party. "You *can* get up, can't you?"

"Well…"

"Because, if not, I'm sure I can find a knight or two to drag you aside." She struggled not to answer his twinkle with a smile, but it was hopeless.

"M'lady, I'll be happy to oblige…if you favor me with a kiss first."

She straightened up and backed away before she gave in to temptation. If her long skirt hadn't tangled around her feet, she would've given him a good swift kick in the…armor. "I will *not*."

"'Tis but a small thing I ask to restore me."

"I'll get the rope off Grandpa's saddle and 'restore' you to the back of the crowd."

His gauntleted hand landed over his heart. "Ah, m'lady, you wound me."

"Don't tempt me" was her reply, though she had to bite her tongue to keep from laughing. Honestly, were all knights so irrepressible?

I mean, she caught herself, *had they been, centuries ago?* Good heavens, her mother was worried about the wrong Ravenwood getting caught up in this knight business.

Behind and all around her, the crowd spoke out in William's favor. "Give 'im a kiss, lady."

"Lay one on 'er, buddy."

"Yeah, you're a lord. Get up and go for it."

William held his helmet up to her. She took it—only to help get him on his way, of course. It was warm in her hands, and she wondered whether it was from the sun...or heated by his body. Distracted, she was a prime target.

As he rose in front of her, she marveled at how tall he was, how broad his chest, how wide his shoulders. While she tried to focus, to rationalize that the metal only made him appear so large and masculine, her face cooled as he leaned in and shadowed her from the sun. Then heated again as his lips covered hers. Stunned, she couldn't move away. Didn't want to.

Now *that* was body heat.

"Good Lord," she whispered.

"'Tis 'my' lord," he gently corrected as he tugged at the helmet clutched in her hands. Once he had it, he jumped onto the back of the moving carriage, flashing her an unrepentant grin as he rolled by.

If she'd found a man that kissed like that four months ago, she wouldn't have been able to help herself—she would've gotten pregnant the conventional way.

THE WEDDING TOOK PLACE in the family chapel—the Marsh family, not these blasted impostors. Until he could find Chelsie, William bided his time doing what all good warriors do—observing.

The myriad of men's and ladies' fashions amused

him for a while. The pointy toes on some of the knights' armor were downright ludicrous.

Conversation afterward was the same as he expected to hear at any gathering: farming, babies, the market. Only after he listened for a while, the market didn't sound quite the same. No one spoke of peddlers, sugar from Spain, or wine from France.

The incident with the old man and his "gun"— William assumed that was the new term for it—were mentioned repeatedly; 'twas to be expected.

What he didn't expect to hear was unbridled praise for Livvy preserving the castle in "a practical manner."

Preposterous! Everyone who held that opinion was as misguided as Edward, as crazy as the old man and as greedy as every Leopold who'd walked the earth. William's fingers cramped on the hilt of his sword in an effort to restrain himself. He wanted to throw everyone out of his castle—except Livvy—but, if he did so, he'd never learn anything about this strange new world.

Or was it a new place? According to Sarah, it might be a new era, but William couldn't believe one theory any more than the other. But then, black magic didn't have to make sense.

At Livvy's invitation, the guests adjourned to the great hall for the wedding feast. 'Twas peculiar how people stroked his armor as they walked past. When Chelsie arrived with a contingent of children, he knew he was in for more of the same, and probably at a price that would weigh her down.

She winked up at him, and none too subtly. "Hi, Lord William."

"At last! I've searched everywhere for you."

"These are my friends. They want to see your sword."

"Let them take their seats now. You and I will sit together and talk."

"It'll only take a second."

"But—"

"I *promised* them," she said through tight lips that reminded him of Livvy. "And you promised to tell them a story about your sword." She turned to her friends and smiled radiantly. "He can be *so* difficult. Watch your fingers."

The children's hands flew behind their backs.

"Chelsie," William admonished, "'tis nonsense. I'd never hurt an innocent child."

A tall boy shoved her. "You said he hacked out a girl's tongue. I want my money back."

William leaned down in the lad's face. "But what I do with impertinent boys is another matter entirely." He made a slow grab for the boy's arm, giving him plenty of time to make his escape and think he was lucky to do so. "Now, miss, what would you have me do for the rest of your friends?"

"Well…"

"Make it quick. You and I have much to discuss."

A small boy peered out from behind a taller girl. "Is…is that the sword you used?"

William stood upright, his hand resting proudly on the jeweled hilt at his side. "This sword has traveled the continents with me. It has served me well through many battles."

He and the children were beginning to draw adult attention.

"Um—" Chelsie glanced nervously over her

shoulder "—better let them touch it now and get to their tables."

William studied her through narrowed eyes. "Then you'll dine with me and answer all my questions?"

She nodded eagerly and made waving motions with her hands, which he assumed meant he should hurry.

"Very well." He drew his sword, and the children fell back. He bent down on one knee, extended the hilt toward them and urged them closer with a smile. He was horribly out of practice at it, but they seemed reassured somewhat as they inched toward him.

Chelsie hovered beside him. He couldn't feel her small hand land on his shoulder, but he knew it was there.

"You'd make a cool father," she said softly, reminding him of his own gentle daughter before the plague had taken her life.

"Chelsie Anne Ravenwood!"

"Uh-oh."

Livvy swished onto the scene in a flurry of skirts, sending children back to their parents, and families to their tables, before she faced off with her daughter. "Did you take money from those children?"

Chelsie nodded.

"You pay back every coin before they leave this hall."

"But what about my expenses?"

The high arch of Livvy's eyebrows amused William as she replied, "It's called absorbing your losses, kid."

When Chelsie glanced at him in a silent plea for help, he carefully remained neutral.

"Now," Livvy continued, "it's almost time to eat. Come sit at the table."

"But I want to eat with Lord William."

"No way."

"Please, m'lady." William sheathed his sword in its silver-engraved scabbard and waited for her to comply with his wishes. 'Twas expected.

"Not only may you two not eat together, you are to stay away from each other. Understand?"

"But, *Mo-om.*"

"M'lady!"

She aimed a smile up at him, all the more disarming due to its suspect sweetness. "That's just it, William. I'm not your lady. Excuse us."

She took Chelsie by the hand and whisked her away, leaving William to stare at her retreating figure and wish for her to slip into that leg-baring costume she'd worn when they'd first met.

Surely she knew he was no danger to a mere child. Knights lived by a code, after all.

He still needed answers. He wanted to know what world he had been cast into, and whether Edward was here also. He wanted to know how Marsh Castle had fallen into her grandfather's hands. He wanted to understand how men could hold fire at their fingertips, light dials on their arms and make music out of the air.

Forget the voice on the little black box. He wasn't ready to understand *that.*

If Livvy wouldn't allow him to speak with her daughter, then Livvy would have to help him. Tonight. In her room, if need be.

LIVVY WORKED the great hall, flitting from person to person and family to family until all were seated at the long tables in the great hall. When someone said,

"Wonderful wedding, Mrs. Ravenwood," she had a response ready.

"I'm so glad you enjoyed it," she said with her brightest, friendliest, yet very businesslike smile as she took her seat beside Chelsie on the bench. "If you know anyone who's planning a wedding, please tell them to keep Marsh Castle in mind."

She was ready when anyone praised her renovations, too. "We think it'll make a nice bed-and-breakfast. Comfortable, you know? A nice blend of the old and the new." Everyone agreed.

Except William. He stalked the room, listening, scowling. His act earned him wide grins and much elbow jabbing between the guests. They chuckled, whispered to each other and laughed together. Occasionally they sparred with William verbally.

She'd been right; he was the hit of the party. For that, she forgave him anything and everything. If enough people wanted to book receptions and parties at Marsh Castle, she'd have to see about putting him on retainer.

He halted behind her, and when she noticed the guests' smiles, she wondered what he was up to. Whatever it was, she'd play along.

"M'lady?"

She craned her neck and tilted her head to gaze up at him. "Yes, Lord William?"

"I have been gone some years. Has custom changed so much that the lord no longer kisses his guests before the meal?"

Certain she flushed a flaming red, she swore if she could send him back a few centuries, she'd do so. Then again, she could give him more than he bargained for—a dose of his own medicine.

She rose, not fooling herself into believing for a moment that she was calling his bluff. One look at his proud face, and she knew he was enjoying every second playing his part. Trouble was, she wasn't an actress and hadn't asked for *this* part.

"No, m'lord," she said, bubbling over inside with the effort not to smile in anticipation of embarrassing the clod. "Times haven't changed so much." She smiled at her guests for effect. "Men usually wait until after dinner now, but we'll do it your way."

She held her hands behind her back—better not to tempt herself—and presented her cheek for his kiss, trying to appear very proper and chaste, trying to throw him off guard. When he grasped her arms with a firm grip, she didn't struggle. When he leaned in and brushed her cheek with his, she could sense every female heart in the room swoon vicariously.

And that was when she turned her lips up to his, when she tilted her head and rose up on tiptoe to reach him better. When she forgot she was doing this to embarrass him and wound her hands behind his neck.

His hair was thick, a mixture of coarse and soft. The rich texture sucked her fingers right in until they were threaded through it, until they cupped the back of his head and pressed him closer.

The applause, thank God, broke the spell. Livvy snatched her hands back to her side and gripped her skirt to keep them where they belonged.

William, the nervy man, *bowed* to the guests and strutted away like a rooster.

"Your lordship," Livvy said, not through with him yet.

He turned. "M'lady?"

"I thought you said it was custom to welcome the guests with a kiss." There were about two hundred more.

"M'lady, if all the guests kiss like that, I shan't have the strength to eat." With a twinkle in his eyes, he turned amidst the laughter and proceeded to the head table.

Livvy cursed her luck at trying to best a comic.

"What's this?" William demanded as he picked up the glass of champagne in front of the bride. "These goblets are too inferior for a wedding feast. Where is the cupbearer?"

Livvy made a mental note to have a faux Oscar made up and engraved with William's name.

He grabbed the nearest waiter, who obviously didn't know he was a cupbearer despite his costume, by the scruff of his neck. "Exchange these for the gold goblets in my mother's private stock."

"Y-yessir." The poor man turned to do as bid, then, when William's back was turned, replaced the bride's glass in front of her.

Livvy found herself as entranced by the lift of William's eyebrows as all the other women were—if their sighs were any indication.

"Insolent fool. Guard, take him away."

"How did he see that?" Chelsie asked. "I thought only moms have eyes in the back of their heads."

"Got me," Livvy replied.

"I'll get them myself. You—come with me," William ordered another servant as he strode out of the hall.

THE SERVANT DISAPPEARED quickly enough, but Tom followed on William's heels. "Man, you are something!''

It sounded like a compliment, but William had no time for such frivolities. The date Sarah had given him was still of concern, but it would seem daft for him to come right out and ask the young, red-haired man the year. There must be another way to get information.

''Are you from around here, Tom?''

''Oh, yeah. Been here all my life.''

''Are there villages nearby?''

''Looking for some action, huh?'' He playfully slugged William's arm. ''Well, there's Newtown, of course.''

Aha! So he was in the same place. Perhaps.

''Where are we going?''

''To my mother's private pantry. What year were you born?''

''Seventy-eight. Why?''

''Fourteen seventy-eight?''

Tom slugged William in the arm again. ''That's a good one. Fourteen seventy-eight.'' He laughed. ''Imagine, that would make me a time traveler.'' Then, ''Nah, if I were, I'd go backward and be a real knight.''

''Like me?''

''Yeah, like—'' Tom scratched his head. ''Uh, look, William, maybe I ought to warn you that the father of the bride's looking a little cranky this afternoon.''

''Really?''

''It doesn't bode well for Livvy, you know, if you tick him off.''

It wasn't William's intent to cause Livvy grief. Not

indirectly, anyway. "Well, then, using my mother's gold goblets for the bride and groom should appease him. Ah, here it is."

LIVVY HAD PEACE for fifteen minutes, during which time Leo opened the toasts with warm wishes to the bride and groom, the meal began, and music played in the background. A roving photographer did his job quietly and competently. His shots would preserve the memories of this day forever for the bride and groom. A few well-selected copies of his work would give Livvy the publicity photos she needed for the bed-and-breakfast brochure.

When William returned, a black scowl upon his face, a sudden hush fell over the room. He stopped behind Livvy again, forcing her to twist her neck to keep an eye on him.

"M'lady, there is a thief among us. My mother's gold dinner service is missing." He addressed her, but announced it loudly enough to be heard by one and all.

Leo, sitting uptable, wadded up his napkin and threw it down. He scowled at Livvy, who pretended not to see, as she hadn't a clue what to do. But only for a moment.

"I sent it out to be cleaned, m'lord."

William's mouth opened, then snapped shut.

"Have a seat, m'lord. You look a bit pale." *That* was a stretch; the man looked as if he lived in the sun. "Perhaps some food would help."

He glanced at the head table, and she knew instantly he was going to complain about the lord's seat being taken by the groom or someone else. So Livvy popped up, took him by the arm and sat him a few places down the length of her table.

"But, m'lady—"

She picked up a roll and stuck it into his mouth. He yanked it out, started to complain, then gazed at the roll as if he'd never tasted anything so good. She left him there to amuse those sitting around him.

By the time the meal ended and dessert was cleared away, it was quite evident that the guests who had the best time were those seated nearest William. Especially the children. Even Chelsie peeked around the adults and emulated him, which meant she regressed to pouring water from her goblet into the nearest bowl and washing her fingers in it.

Livvy's gaze was caught by Leo, who, with a twitch of his head, indicated she should meet him outside the main door. Which she did.

"Get rid of that insufferable man at once."

"But, Leo—"

He paced the stone floor. "Ordinarily I'm a patient man, but he's making a mockery of my daughter's reception. Need I remind you that her wedding is the most special day I can ever give her? That she's my only child?"

Livvy had to bite her tongue not to tell him her views on the pressures put on only children. If she couldn't find her own Mr. Right, at least she should be able to see to it that Chelsie wouldn't be a single.

"How important this is to your bed-and-breakfast?"

She swallowed her retort about shoving it—William *was* the life of the party—but couldn't risk Leo shoving her loan note in her face.

"Have I made myself clear?"

"Yes, Leo, I'll get rid of him."

She'd never fired anyone in her life, much less tried to send a hulking big knight off the premises. How did one bounce a man who wore steel and carried a sword and an ax? She was still dredging up possible scenarios when the band began and the tables and benches were stacked aside to make room for dancing.

William strolled around the room, checking out the musicians, cocking his head and evaluating the dancers. She lost sight of him in the moving, swaying crowd.

He appeared beside her shoulder. "M'lady."

"I'm afraid I have bad news for you."

"You sold my mother's gold?"

"No!" *He got me.* She grinned up at him. "How do you do that?"

"Do what?"

"Make everyone believe you're for real."

"Because I am."

"Yeah, and I'm Guinevere."

His face grew pensive. "King Arthur's bride?"

"Actually, if I don't get you out of here before Leo loses his temper, I'll be more like Marie Antoinette."

He held out his hand. "M'lady—"

She whirled on him. "Don't make me get tough."

William slowly studied the room. "M'lady, you have men-at-arms to do that for you."

She frowned at his hand, still hanging there between them, then up at him. "What?"

He glanced at the couples swaying on the dance floor, then gazed at her as if she were the only woman in the great hall. His undivided attention, his disregard for any other woman in the room, lit an ember deep inside her.

"I wish to try my hand at that," he said.

"Oh?"

"With you."

"Oh."

He grinned. "I believe you already said that. Does it mean 'aye'?"

She slipped her hand into his, pleased that he'd dispensed with the hard gauntlet, surprised that touching his hand robbed her of the power of speech. Only temporarily, she was sure. It wouldn't take him long to do something for which she'd have to scold him, which seemed futile since she was firing him.

As soon as this dance is over.

She let him lead her onto the dance floor, then found out he still wasn't through playing his part.

He looked around at the other couples, raised his arms, made one attempt to place them like everyone else, then studied the other men and tried again.

"Is this right?" he asked.

She'd wanted to do something more medieval at the reception, but the bride had insisted on traditional, classical music. At the moment, Livvy was glad. "Mmm-hmm."

He swayed, but his feet didn't move.

"Armor too heavy for dancing?"

"I don't know the step yet."

"That's okay. I'll lead." And she did—right for the door.

Halfway across the room, one of the bridesmaids cut in. Livvy found her grandfather and cut in there.

"Grandpa, you've got to help me. I don't know if Leo's mad at the disturbance William made or the fact that he got more laughs at dinner than Leo, but he told me to fire him and get him out of here. Only, I don't know how.''

Her grandfather tugged thoughtfully on his gray moustache, nodded slowly and spoke quietly, as if to himself. ''Yeah, that one could cause trouble, sure enough. I'll round up a posse.''

She rolled her eyes, but let the posse remark slide since he was coming to her rescue.

''Get another dance with him and ease him toward the door.''

''I tried that already. We were waylaid.''

''Keep cutting in until you get 'im there.''

Over the next thirty minutes, Livvy cut in to dance with William no less than ten times. Every time she got him headed toward the door, she lost him again. People were starting to stare.

William took her in his arms again.

Livvy danced with him for a moment before she realized what had changed. ''You're leading.''

''Am I? Where would you like to go?''

''Out for a breath of fresh air.''

He winked at her.

''Don't even think it.''

He pulled her close to his breastplate and twirled until she had no choice but to lift her feet off the floor or look stupid trying to keep up. They made the door successfully that time, and he gently cupped her elbow and led her outside.

''Now!'' her grandfather ordered the four knights with him.

William pushed Livvy behind him. ''Run, m'lady! I'll hold them off.''

He reached for his sword and barely had it out of

the scabbard when a knight brushed past Livvy and hit William on the back of the head. As Livvy yelled her objection to throwing him out with undue force, William turned and backhanded his assailant against the wall. In the next few seconds, there was a general piling-on of armored knights, much like pro football, and William was dragged off.

Though, from repeated sounds of metal crunching against stone as they retreated out of sight, Livvy suspected William wasn't getting the worst of it.

5

THE DUNGEON seemed smaller to William than it had when he'd been a child, when he and his brother had made a game of locking each other in to see if it was escape-proof. While an actual prisoner never escaped with his head intact, he and Edward always found their way out sooner or later. Of course, they'd been smaller then.

And it smelled a whole lot better now than then.

After spending the night in camp with the other knights and all their magical gadgets, he was convinced he had somehow been cast into a different world. After talking to Sarah and Tom, he had to consider this "time travel" thing. Imagine—the future! But the variety of people at the wedding greatly clouded the issue. Wouldn't fashion have changed more consistently?

How Edward had done it to him, William had no idea. Had he come forward five hundred years? If so, how to go back was a mystery, and the best place to tackle it was in his father's study, not in a cramped cell at the bottom of a tower.

No guard had been posted to hear him loosen the stones in the corner of the cell, down low. 'Twould take a larger hole than when he'd been in his youth, and he scraped and pried and tugged diligently into the night. He was prepared to work until dawn, if need be, but, in the dark, he felt a metal object behind the third stone he dug out.

Unable to see his find, he traced it with the tips of his fingers and discovered 'twas a key.

"Well, Edward, you cheat," he murmured as he made use of it. "So that's how you always got out so fast."

The cell door swung open stiffly. He groped his way around the anteroom, recovered his sword and poleax near the door and silently crept out of the dungeon. He didn't need a candle to know there were twenty-four narrow steps winding up to the courtyard. Moonlight gave him good reason to move stealthily through the shadows until he entered the castle.

Unfortunately no one had blown out the candles in the wall sconces after the revelry. He blew at one only to find it didn't so much as waver. Trapped inside a clear shell, the candlelight shone outward and threatened his safety. He drew his sword and, with one smooth swing, chopped the magic candle off at the base.

Instant darkness—if he didn't count the sparks. More magic.

Livvy could explain this to him along with everything else. While thoughts of her lying in bed, her hair unbound, drew him toward her, the possibility of going back from where he'd come gave him good reason to visit his father's study first—the place where it had all begun.

He had to hack off several more candles on the way, which turned out to be foolish because, when he got to the study, he could have used some light. No ordinary candle was about—a very strange way to live; in the light when it should be night, in the dark when he wanted to find a clue as to what had happened to him. It was a futile effort in the dark.

Since there were no guards about, he refrained from putting out any more candles in the passages as he headed toward the one where he'd seen Livvy backing out of Chelsie's room the evening before. With no signs of a governess, he figured Livvy would be sleeping nearby.

He was just passing Chelsie's door when she opened it, winked at him and retreated into her room.

He could, of course, follow her and ask his questions. That had been his original plan, as she seemed the friendliest person around. But the thought of Livvy lying in bed, her golden waves tumbling across the pillow, her face soft in sleep, was much more enticing.

If he was going to get answers, why not get them from the sweetest place?

He opened several doors, all of which led to unoccupied rooms. He had one to go, and he'd left it until last because it seemed most unbelievable that she'd be sleeping in his room. But she was. He couldn't see her, but he heard her soft breathing and inhaled the same exotic scent that had mingled with her hair when they'd danced.

Slowly his eyes adjusted to the moonlight spilling in through the window, across the floor, up the side of the bed. His bed—he'd recognize the headboard anywhere, even if he hadn't carved his initials in it during his sixth winter.

Slowly Livvy's body beneath the sheet took form. If he concentrated long enough, he could see the rise and fall of her ribs as she breathed the breath of sleep. Her head moved from side to side, as if dreaming, and she moaned softly. It seemed a shame to wake her for a few answers. An hour's time would make little difference one way or t'other.

Little difference for some things, anyway. For other matters, an hour could be filled with an eternity of pleasure. The thought was too much to bear, too strong to oppose. He'd been without a warm woman too long. Livvy was no innocent maiden. He was a lord; she would welcome his attention.

Removing his armor in the dark, without a squire's assistance, was a slow process in the interest of silence. His clothes and padding fell to the floor as he strode to the bed. First he would pleasure her—then she would answer his questions.

LIVVY HADN'T HAD such sweet dreams in years, but then she hadn't ever met a knight before. The shining armor bit didn't fit, as William's was quite discolored, but she'd caught a twinkle in his gray eyes that made up for it—in her dreams.

In the safety of sleep, she was free to put him back up on his white charger, to let her gaze roam over his broad shoulders, to wonder what muscles lay beneath his armor. While she was at it, she added a long, flowing gown for herself and had him pull her up onto the horse and settle her, *oh so intimately,* across his thighs.

Her imagination went into overdrive again. Why, she could *feel* his arms around her, tugging her, pulling her against his chest, gently fondling her breasts. His palms were calloused—that seemed to be a lot of detail for a dream, but she wasn't about to quit now— and his work-roughened skin threw her sensory nerve endings into a frenzy of longing.

Her conscience screamed, *I don't want just sex. I want Mr. Right*. But that kind of reality had no place in her dreams, so she resolutely shoved it aside, just as he was doing with the covers.

Cool air feathered across her skin. Warm hands followed, tracing a path downward, pausing to tease her navel.

"Mmm," she murmured, burrowing her hips into the man behind her to egg him on. Bare skin touched bare skin. *On board a horse?*

Never mind.

Her dream came to an abrupt end when her knight jumped off the bed, sputtering, "You're with child," as if it were an offensive notion.

She switched on the bedside lamp and blinked until she got him in focus, hoping it wasn't really her knight-for-hire. The covers were down around her knees, her gown up around her neck.

Talk about a nightmare.

"William?" Another blink, and she whipped the blanket up to her collarbone.

"M'lady, if only I'd known of your condition—"

"My—" She looked around for something to throw at him. "It's *your* condition that's in danger here."

He glanced at the door. "You have a lover?"

"No."

His gaze seared her covered torso, which gave her time to check out what he'd been hiding beneath his armor.

Whoa, baby!

"Then you are recently widowed. Again, my apologies, m'lady."

As big and broad as he was, she figured he filled

every cubic inch of his suit or armor—and very nicely, indeed.

She remembered not to drool.

BY WILLIAM'S COUNT, the lady had been widowed a very short time. Her belly had been rounded beneath his palm, but hadn't shown beneath her clothes. Nor had he gotten kicked by a tiny foot, though the babe could be asleep.

Had she been widowed longer, he might have answered the need in her eyes and climbed back into her bed. He searched her face, hoping to find that she hadn't loved her husband, hoping she would open her arms and—

The pillow that smacked into his erection doubled him over.

Then again, maybe she still loved the bastard.

He held the pillow as a shield over his most vital part while he slowly regained his power of speech. "You need a man." His voice was rough and strained.

"And I suppose you're applying for the job?"

He pulled himself up to his full height, took a deep breath to expand his chest and show her that he was a man on whom she could depend. "M'lady, I offer you my protection," he said in a booming voice. He strode to the side of her bed.

She pulled the blanket up to her chin. "I need protection *from* you, not *by* you."

"You refuse me?"

He saw her struggle not to let her gaze drop to his pillow. Her sigh was long and drawn-out. "I'm not looking for a one-night stand."

"I wasn't thinking of standing."

She smiled sadly. "No thanks."

"And I certainly am not going to share you with any other kni—"

"Get out, William."

"M'lady—"

"Out, before I add some new scars to your body. Out of my bedroom, out of my—"

"'Twas my bedchamber long ago."

She rolled her eyes, a most endearing sight.

"If you refuse me, m'lady, I shall find you another."

"Out."

He tossed the pillow onto the bed and turned away until he was decently covered again. "You must have a husband."

She grimaced and took a very deep breath. "You sound like my mother."

"She's wise to understand that a woman alone is prey to unscrupulous men."

"Yeah? What about unscrupulous husbands and philandering fiancés?"

He would not be deterred. "Especially one in your condition."

"Then heaven save me from wise people. Especially my mother, who has enough worry for six more kids."

"Mothers are like that."

"I don't expect you to understand. *You* have a brother."

Somewhere.

So, the lady wasn't as willing as William had hoped. Back to the business of where—or *when*—he was.

"What year is this?"

"Oh, William, give it up, will you?"

"Please, m'lady, I must know."

Her eyebrows drew together in a delicate pucker. "Do you have amnesia or something? Oh my God—" she rose up onto her knees, gripping the cover above her breasts, giving him a tantalizing glimpse of creamy shoulders "—did you hit your head when you fell off Grandpa's horse?"

"I did not fall off!"

Her answering laugh was light. "Oh, okay."

Too late, he realized maybe he should have agreed. If he admitted to a head wound, would she cradle him to her breast to comfort him? He would find out, after he got the information he needed.

"Please, m'lady…"

She sat back on the mattress with a long, drawn-out sigh. "Nineteen ninety-eight. I could call a doctor, I suppose."

Five hundred years! 'Twas impossible that Sarah, Tom and Livvy were all mistaken.

Small, unsteady steps carried him to her bedside, where he slumped onto the mattress. "Are you certain?"

She eased away to the center of the bed, pulling her blanket with her. "What are you doing?"

"My head…" He touched the back of his skull and winced theatrically. "I think someone hit me."

He was rewarded with a tender gaze. "I'm sorry. I had no idea Grandpa was going to sic all those knights on you. Is it bleeding?"

"I…I don't know." He strove to sound weak, which wasn't too far off the mark sitting so close and knowing honor wouldn't allow him to touch her without her permission. "Maybe you should send for a physician."

"Turn around."

He was happy to do so, if only to hide his grin—which disappeared the moment she ran her fingers through his hair. "Ah."

"Doesn't sound too painful." She thumped him right on the lump.

"Ow." He turned to see if her blanket had slipped, if he could glimpse more than a creamy shoulder, but luck had deserted him.

"Get off my bed."

How he would like to stay. No...how he would like to be *allowed* to stay.

"M'lady, I beg your patience. I'm a stranger to this time, and I have many questions."

Her brows quirked. "Does that line work on *anyone?*"

"Not yet." He growled his frustration. "Have you no compassion for a weary traveler?"

"Sure. You can bed down with the rest of the knights outside the castle wall."

He feared time was short. How could he fathom when Edward's black magic would renew itself?

He couldn't—not for certain. But he did know Livvy was a pregnant woman alone, and she needed the protection of a man. If he could count on being there for her, he would pursue her, court her, win her.

But he couldn't, not until he understood if the curse would wrench him away again, so he left her side. 'Twas the honorable thing to do.

He gathered up his padding and armor. "I might have to leave soon." There was no way of knowing when. "I'll work diligently, night and day, to find you a husband before I go. I give you my word."

6

LIVVY LAY IN BED in the dark, wishing William's visit had, indeed, been a dream. Then she could close her eyes and enjoy it, savor his touch, feel his warm body behind her, relive the way he'd aroused her.

He was all temptation, whether he was clanking around her castle in a tarnished old suit of armor or standing naked and hard behind a pillow. He'd be gone in the morning, along with all the other knights who paled beside him. After all, he'd no longer be on her payroll; he'd return to his day job.

In a way, it was a pity he had to go. He was certainly dashing. Everyone liked him. Everyone except Leo. But since his daughter's wedding had been a success, Livvy no longer had to worry about him on that account.

But if her real Mr. Right ever found her, at least he'd be able to stay on a horse and wouldn't jabber nonsense about being a stranger to this time. Honestly, William sounded like her grandfather.

She fell asleep laughing about his tumble, wondering how he'd gotten the half-dozen scars scattered over his chest, memorizing the location of every one of them. She woke up in another sweat as she relived, over and over, the kiss he'd given her just before he'd jumped onto the wedding carriage.

She'd have to control her dangerously overactive

imagination. Better to throw herself back into renovations and get the bed-and-breakfast open on sched-
ule. After all, she'd come here on a mission to find
some cousins *and* to avoid her mother's wearisome
concern. Livvy had to earn a living so she could stay.

The interruption of the wedding had been a costly
delay. She hoped there'd be no others.

A CHILLY, ROSE-STREAKED dawn brought new insight
to William. 'Twas important that he fit in this unusual
century for as long as he was present and, since he
saw no one in armor when he opened his eyes, he set
about studying their unusual clothing and where he
might obtain some.

He also remembered his oath to find a suitable husband for Livvy, a man who would protect her and be
a good father to her children.

But who was going to want to take on a pregnant
woman—and a daughter with pecuniary interests to
rival the national treasury? Some of the knights he'd
sat with the evening before might have been suitable,
but they were already packing up camp.

With a hip stiff and sore from yesterday's tumble
and doing his best to disguise a limp, William ven-
tured over to the laborers' camp on the far side of
Marsh Castle. They had no tents and lean-tos, but
much more stable structures on wheels.

'Twas there he found fashionable clothing: a set of
sturdy breeches that continued right on up his back,
ending in straps that crossed his shoulders and hooked
to a similar piece in front.

"What do you call this?" he asked the nearest
man.

The reply came with a skeptical frown. "I dunno. Clean?"

"Aye, but clean what?"

"Uh, clean and fresh?" he said over his shoulder as he left.

Under that, most men wore shirts of the softest knit, with short sleeves. Their helmets were hard enough, he supposed, though only the top of his head would be protected. What good was half a helmet without a visor? For that matter, what good was a helmet without body armor?

He dressed quickly in a white shirt and the faded blue, clean and fresh whatevers. Over all, he buckled on his belt and sword. One could never be too careful.

A meaty hand landed on his shoulder. Always at the ready, he grasped his sword, but did not draw it.

"Helluva fall you took yesterday," the laborer said in a friendly fashion.

William grimaced, both at the pain in his hip and at the humiliation of falling in front of Livvy. "If I'd had my own horse, I wouldn't have been unseated."

The man's grin was broad. "Yeah, but look what you got for your trouble."

William nodded, feeling his own lips tug into a smile at the memory of Livvy's soft, sun-kissed skin. "Aye, there's that."

He winked and elbowed William. "I guess the knights are still getting the ladies, huh? You been doing this long?"

William wasn't sure what he meant.

"You know—wearing armor. Have you been doing it long?"

"As near as I can figure, five hundred years."

"Uh-huh. Okay." He took a deep breath and

scratched his head just below the back edge of his open helmet. "Whatever. But," he said as he walked away, "don't you think a sword on the work site's a bit much?"

William discarded the man's concern as trivial compared to his own. If he suddenly flew through time again—Edward's magic was strong, and who knew how far it reached?—he didn't want to be without his sword. He wasn't certain whether 'twas bravery or foolishness that had him walking around without his armor.

He followed the workers into the castle, knowing these were not the same laborers who had been camped outside Marsh Castle when he'd left. The amount of destruction they'd already wreaked was a hundredfold worse than he could have imagined. Their tools were damned noisy, buzzing, whirring gadgets that made short work of an ancient wall here and cut timbers for a new one there.

"You—what's your name?" a man bellowed. He had a long roll of paper in his hand and pointed it at William.

"Lord William."

"Ah, yes, I heard about you." He sounded like George, whom William had heard, but not seen. "You're that knight fellow who thinks this here's his castle, right?"

"Aye, Marsh Castle and all the land surrounding it are mine."

"Yeah, and I'm the king of England. Get to work."

'Twould not do to get thrown out of his own castle, so William turned and joined three men huddled over a wooden beam. He scrutinized each one closely.

None smelled of spirits nor was too ugly to bear, not that Livvy could afford to be choosey.

"Are any of you unwed?" he asked.

Their conversation stopped immediately. A look flashed among them, too fast for William to interpret, but then two of them held up their left hands, each displaying a simple gold band.

"I'm looking for a man who would make a good husband," William explained.

The third one held up both hands. "Hey, I'm spoken for."

William nodded. "Can you—?"

They deserted him promptly, before he could even make known his request. Could they know what he was about? Had someone else already searched for a husband for Livvy?

Maybe she was a shrew.

He was more circumspect when he approached the next workman, who held a tool in front of him that sawed through timber noisily—and in the blink of an eye. He wore no ring.

"How does that work?" William asked, employing a more subtle approach this time.

"Huh?" The laborer paused, silenced his tool and lifted a pitifully small, clear visor up until it rested on his forehead. Why, the thing was so tiny, a man could lose his whole jaw in the first moments of battle. "Couldn't hear you."

"Can you explain this tool to me? What makes the noise? What makes it work so fast?" *How the blazes do I kill it?*

"Get off my cord. I got work to do." He tugged at the smooth line beneath William's feet.

William traced it and many others to a common

source—a metal box bolted to the wall. Beyond that, he couldn't understand how it worked, nor could he detect whether there was a source beyond it. But, as he walked around, he realized if he didn't make them stop working on his castle, soon there wouldn't be anything left of his ancestral home at all.

"Stop!" he bellowed, but 'twas drowned out by all the noise. He strode up to a carpenter measuring a thick board, drew his sword and neatly bisected the wood right on the mark.

The çarpenter jumped back as the two halves clattered to the stone floor. One by one, nearby tools whirred down to silence.

"What the hell'd you do that for?"

"To get your attention."

"Well, you got it."

William's gaze traveled the room, noting everyone in it. "You will all cease using these tools immediately."

One grinned. "You issuing swords instead?"

Another chuckled. "I always listen to the man with the biggest weapon. Just how thick a board will that thing go through?"

William was pleased to make short work of their available timber—that would mean fewer changes in his castle—and the more men that gathered around him, the happier he was to take up the challenge, which grew into a rather spirited contest. Until Livvy arrived.

"What the hell is going on?" Her angelic voice was raised to a demanding pitch, and the men parted to let her through.

"M'lady."

When she saw him at the center of attention, her

groan was most enticingly feminine. "I should have known." She stepped over a cartload of severed boards lying about. "Where's my foreman?"

As George shuffled his feet and ducked behind several others, William grinned, pleased to see he'd corrupted even him.

"Get back to work," she ordered all of them.

"But I just got them to stop," William said.

"That won't happen again."

"It won't?"

"I can't believe this is your day job." She hung her head momentarily, then looked him in the eye. "You're fired. I'd have you thrown in the dungeon, but apparently you're an escape artist, too."

"You can't fire me."

"I just did." Her smile was sugary sweet. If her foot tapping on the stone floor meant the same thing as when his mother used to do it—and apparently it did, as the men returned to their stations and started their tools one by one—then he had to act fast.

"I don't work for you," he said quite reasonably as he strode across the room to the metal box.

With battle-honed muscles, he raised his arm and thrust his sword into the source of the workers' power. Sparks flew; his sword clattered to the stone; hissing and spitting petered into silence. He was sure his smile was quite smug.

"And neither do they."

INSTEAD OF SPARKS, Livvy saw dollar signs. Big, fat, red ones.

"That's a wrap," George told his crew, who immediately headed for the door like a pack of deserters.

"Wait," Livvy beseeched. It was that or take a

two-by-four to William. "Come back. It can be fixed." They hovered around the doorway as she turned to George for confirmation. "Can't it?"

"I'll get an electrician right on it, but it'll take a couple days."

"Days?" She slumped onto a sawhorse.

"The whole castle's probably out. If you want hot meals, Cheshire Inn down in the village is good."

William positively gloated. "Aye, dine in the village."

She aimed a smug smile at him. "We'll be fine here. I'm sure we'll live through a cold meal or two."

"You've ruined most of my castle," William said, "but there are many fireplaces yet. You may cook in them."

Livvy laughed at the thought. "That went out with the Middle Ages."

"Ah," William said with a maddening grin, "then 'tis lucky I am here. I know how to do these things."

"Thanks, but I'll manage without you."

"There's a cold front moving in," George warned. "Nothing I can do about the heat. Maybe you should let him stay and get some fires laid."

"Aye," he agreed, as devastatingly sexy in overalls as he had been in armor.

"What are you?" Livvy asked.

"I beg your pardon?"

"Are you a carpenter?"

"No, m'lady."

"An electrician?"

"What is an electrician?"

She tipped her head toward the damaged electrical box. "Someone who could fix that."

"No, m'lady. But I can organize the men to gather firewood and, if you need meat, I can hunt."

She could only shake her head at him. She'd like to throttle him, but knew better than to touch him again. "I have two words for you."

"M'lady?"

"Seek help."

"Aye." He looked entirely too pleased as he turned toward the men still hovering around the door. "You!" he barked. "Yes, you. How many of you have wives and families waiting for you at home?" Most of them raised their hands, and they were quickly dismissed. "The rest of you, come with me."

"Where're we going?"

"To gather firewood, of course."

To Livvy's amazement, none of them bolted for their trucks.

"None of you are wed?" was the last thing she heard William ask as they trooped out of the hall.

Her grandfather ambled in and paused by her side. "I'd hoped he was leaving," he said grimly.

"Me, too," she said, then glanced at his ashen face to see if he could tell she was lying. "Grandpa, are you okay?"

"Yup."

His knuckles were as white as his pearl-handed pistol. "Grandpa," she warned, "you can't shoot the man for riding your horse."

"It ain't the horse I'm worried about."

LIVVY MANAGED to keep busy even without electricity, though she let Sarah off until power could be restored. Sweeping, dusting and window cleaning were still manual jobs. The quiet chores allowed her and Chelsie, sitting on a nearby window seat, to chat undisturbed as a cool breeze freshened the room.

"Wouldn't it be wonderful to marry a knight?" Chelsie asked with a sigh a little too advanced for her age.

The thought wasn't too advanced for Livvy, however. Imagining William to be a real, chivalrous, dragon-slaying knight in shining armor jump-started her libido, made her heart skip a few beats and her knees turn to jelly.

When she noticed she was stroking the woodwork instead of rubbing it clean, she was relieved to see her daughter hadn't noticed.

"I suppose so. If," she said pointedly to Chelsie, "you remember that they lived long ago. Not here. Not now."

But a woman could dream, couldn't she?

"Uh-huh. But as long as William's here and now, we could have a tournament to raise money."

"We're doing fine, honey. The rent-a-knights have gone back to their day jobs. We'll be open for business soon." Livvy hoped some of the guests brought children Chelsie's age so she'd have someone to play with, someone to curb her wild imagination.

Chelsie gazed out the window. "Here comes a car. I think it's Leo."

Glad for the break, Livvy tossed her dust rag aside and held out her hand. "Good." She smiled brightly, hoping to distract Chelsie from her tournament fixation. "Let's go listen to him tell us how wonderful the wedding was."

Without power, the shortcut passages were out of the question, as those routes had no windows to let in daylight, so Livvy chose a circuitous path past a rear door. There, she was amused to see William leading a contingent of men loaded down with firewood.

"M'lady, I shall lay a fire in your chamber and Chelsie's. The rest of this should allow you to cook until the source of power is fixed."

She could have sworn he winked at her, but the movement of his eyelid was so slight, and the room so dim, she couldn't be sure.

"Though I warn you, you must not let the workers do any more damage."

Sunlight streamed in as the door flew open.

"Mrs. Ravenwood," Leo boomed from the doorway, his black brows furrowed together.

Livvy summoned up courage she suddenly wasn't feeling. "Leo," she greeted warmly.

He strode across the stone floor, reached into his vest and pulled out a sheet of paper folded in thirds. "I'm here to give you notice."

Curiosity made her want to accept the paper; dread kept her hands clasped in front of her. "Notice? I'm afraid I don't understand."

"It's very simple, really. My daughter's reception was a disaster. I'm calling in your loan note."

"But, Leo, it was a wonderful party. And we're scheduled to open in less than a month. I've got workers to pay and—"

"By the end of the month, Mrs. Ravenwood."

"The end—" she squeaked. "You want your money in two weeks? That's impossible!"

Leo waved the paper in front of her face. "Pay it, or the castle is mine."

William's growl behind her was so furious, it sounded inhuman.

"Well, it's still mine for now," she snapped. "Get out."

William faced off with Leo. "This castle will never be yours."

Leo bent backward and roared with laughter. He glanced at Livvy, then back to William. "I guess you thought it would be yours, right?"

"'Tis mine already. And if I have to leave here, then 'tis the lady's."

"Wrong, you impudent gigolo."

If Livvy had known William could pick up her bulky neighbor, she would have tried to stop him. As it was, Leo was up in the air, swimming over William's head before she could protest.

"Put me down!"

"I believe the lady told you—" William tossed him out the door and down the steps "—to get out." He brushed his palms together, as if touching Leo had left dirt on his hands.

It took Livvy a moment, but she finally managed to string two words together. "Oh, William, you shouldn't have done that."

"Nonsense. He was rude to you."

"But I owe him money."

"Do you have it?"

"Well, no."

"Then I've done no harm, have I?"

He slung his arm across her shoulders in a gesture that was probably supposed to comfort her, but only confused her further. Much further.

"I...guess not."

"He can't collect what you don't have."

"But the castle is collateral."

"M'lady, the castle is mine."

With a simple squeeze of his arm, she realized he'd just thrown a man out of the castle for her. If it had been five hundred years earlier, she guessed that would be considered romantic.

Heck, this was the end of the twentieth century, and her heart was thinking it was romantic now.

WILLIAM WAS CONVINCED that Leo was a descendant of the blasted Leopold clan. The resemblance was too uncanny to be otherwise. Even the name. Aye, and he remembered the coat of arms on the wedding banners. 'Twas the same family, sure enough.

Livvy was in no mood to answer his questions, the number of which increased hourly. Though she wasn't as distraught as his wife would have been, she was, nonetheless, in a stew.

"See? I'm right," Chelsie said to William as Livvy walked away, shoulders slumped.

"About what?"

"We need to have a tournament, 'cause now Mom doesn't have any money and we'll lose the castle to Leo and have to go back to the U.S. and—"

"Silence." He couldn't think with all her chattering.

On one hand, if they left, he'd have his castle back. On the other, he'd miss Livvy. And he hadn't done his duty yet and seen her settled with a husband.

"—live in a crummy old apartment and be *bored to death* and breathe smog—"

He might even miss Chelsie, he realized with wonder. "How will a tournament help?"

"I'll sell tickets. We'll make money," she said matter-of-factly. "Programs, too, and refreshments—"

"Did your father not teach you any manners, child?"

She shook her head. "I don't remember him."

Her mother was no more than a few months along. "Your uncle then."

Chelsie grinned slyly, as if she'd heard the innuendo before. "Nope, no *uncle,* either. My mom got pregnant in a lab."

"What word is this?"

"It's a place where they have a sperm bank."

7

SUDDENLY, William didn't want to discuss anything with a precocious, eight-year-old child. He needed Livvy, and he needed her *now*.

"Women go there to get pregnant."

"Silence!" At her startled look, he added, more gently, "Tell me how this is possible. No, never mind."

He'd let Livvy do that, though he couldn't believe a woman as beautiful as she had to go to a "lab" place to be bedded by a stranger. What was wrong with the old-fashioned way? It must be her sassy mouth. Very unattractive.

And yet...very refreshing. "Tell me why."

"'Cause my mom didn't have very good luck with men in Illinois, and she says she's glad she did it 'cause she wants me to have at least one brother or sister, and all the men over here are put off by my great-grandpa."

William marveled that an eight-year-old understood all that and he could only pretend to, but he made some sense of it, having met the old man. And Livvy.

"I see." The situation strengthened his resolve to find her a responsible husband—with great haste. The spouse in question must be a man who could provide for and protect Livvy and her little girl. And the babe, of course.

William wondered if it would be another little girl, with blond hair and blue eyes and freckles. If she would look like Livvy, or totally different.

No, this was just too confusing! How did men in this time put up with such nonsense?

If only Livvy hadn't refused him. If only he knew whether he was destined to stay. If only he could help her before he had to go.

"You think a tournament will help?"

Chelsie's eyes grew round, as if she sensed a willing accomplice. "A tournament—oh, yes. We can—"

"Silence. Let me think."

A tournament would bring knights from miles around. Unwed men who might overlook a little indiscretion in favor of a beautiful, blue-eyed, golden-haired vision. Though the thought of her warming another man's bed didn't set well with him, he knew 'twas his duty as lord to see to her welfare if she would not.

"I'll help you with a plaisance." There was no sense putting on a tournament to draw a worthy knight and then maiming or killing the man before William could see him safely wed to Livvy.

Chelsie's eyebrows puckered in a little frown, and William was pleased that he'd been able to outwit her in *something*.

"What's a plaisance?"

"'Tis for show only, with blunted weapons. Come, we will talk about it while I hunt."

LIVVY SLAMMED STONEWARE plates onto the kitchen table with a clatter that threatened to crack them.

Four, in case William returned with meat. After all, even though she could have defrosted something—if he'd given her time to explain, which he hadn't—she couldn't very well let the man hunt for supper, then send him away hungry.

Though why she should give his stomach a second thought was beyond her. If his actions represented chivalry, no wonder it had failed. Where was a dragon-slaying knight when she really needed one?

She banged a glass down at each place setting, then slapped knives and forks beside the plates. She yanked cloth napkins out of a drawer and turned around just in time to see William holding two dead mammals out at arm's length, as if they were trophy fish, beneath her nose.

She fled backward until she smacked her tailbone against a cabinet. "What the heck are those?"

She ignored his reply. Chelsie's face was smeared with an awful lot of reddish brown dirt for a short afternoon in the woods. Livvy leaned down for a closer look and brushed some blond tendrils out of Chelsie's eyes, tucking them behind her ear.

"Did you fall?"

"No." Chelsie not only looked insulted, she sounded it, too.

Then she looked at William and they were all smiles; apparently they'd had a ball rounding up supper together.

Chelsie turned back to Livvy. "It's hare's blood."

Yu-uck!

Livvy must have misunderstood. She *hoped* she'd misunderstood. "It's what?"

"Hare's blood," Chelsie said matter-of-factly.

"You know," William said, "for the freckles."

"No, I don't know," Livvy said slowly and distinctly. "And—" she held up her hand to stop him from speaking "—I don't want to know."

"Hare's blood bleaches freckles out, Mommy. William says so."

"We might not have done it right, though," he admitted with a slight tilt of his head to one side, which, in Livvy's estimation, only served to emphasize his sexy, crooked smile. "My wife used to handle such matters."

Her heart stopped for a moment, and she refused to analyze why. Her mouth didn't, though. "Your wife?"

"Yes, m'lady. 'Twas the womenfolk who handled such matters in my time, though Chelsie assures me 'tis not that way now."

"You're married?"

She'd have sworn he was still playacting, but no one could affect the dark look of pain that filled his eyes and erased his smile.

"Nay. My wife and child died."

"Oh." At a loss for words, she offered the best she could. "I'm sorry."

"'Twas long ago, m'lady."

"They had the plague," Chelsie explained, totally unfazed by the concept of death. "In the fifteenth century. They bleached freckles with hare's blood—"

William held the hares up again, proudly.

"—and they didn't have trucks."

"Aye, the trucks!" William's eyes grew as round as Chelsie's did on occasion, and his whole body was animated with the excitement of it all. "I watched the workers leave in them. No horses to water or feed, just power. I never imagined I'd see such a grand sight. Though I wish they'd camped outside the wall again." His face grew pensive. "I had unfinished business with them."

"Yeah, me, too, but you don't see me smearing my face with blood."

"I think our business is different," he said vaguely.

"Chelsie, honey, wash your face."

"He's a time traveler, Mom. I explained it to him."

"He is not." Not that her traitorous body didn't *want* him to be a real knight. "And use plenty of soap."

"But I might have to leave it on overnight."

Livvy grabbed her by the hand, led her to the sink and turned on the water. Out of habit, she waited for it to warm and, while she did so, she rounded on William, the instigator. "And as for you—"

"By the saints!" William stared at the running water.

Chelsie grinned at him. "See, I told you."

"Wash," Livvy ordered, though she was having great difficulty not snickering at their antics.

"But, *Mo-om,* it's cold."

Ah, yes, no electricity yet. "Blame William."

Chelsie obediently stuck her hands under the faucet. "It's okay. I can pretend I'm in the fifteenth century."

"For that, you'd have to go out and draw water," William told her. He leaned down and peered at Livvy's cheeks. "How did you make your freckles disappear?"

"I..."

He was far too close, smelled of fresh air and sunshine, but she had nowhere left to go. She ignored his steel gray irises, and the tiny, puckered scar that rode next to his left eye. Though it wasn't easy.

"I never had any."

"No?"

"And don't change the subject."

"Have I done so?" He looked innocent enough.

"Yes." She bit her lip to keep from smiling. No sense encouraging the man. "Quit filling her head with stories of time travel. And get those dead rabbits out of my kitchen."

"They are hares, m'lady."

"They're dead."

"Aye, I know. I've brought them in for you to skin."

Livvy blinked. "It's not the hares I'm thinking of skinning."

WILLIAM FELT OUT OF PLACE tending the hares as they roasted on a spit in the fireplace. He was unaccustomed to doing servant's work, but there was no one about who indicated that this was inappropriate. 'Twas not that he *couldn't* do it—in the past six years away from his home, the job had fallen to him as often as not out of necessity.

Without a servant now, though, the job should have fallen to Livvy, but she, standing with her back to him, had her hands under a seemingly endless stream of water.

"What are you doing?" he asked.

"Thinking of ways to trip you up."

"M'lady, I am quite surefooted."

Her shoulders rose and fell on a sigh. "I'm cleaning potatoes so you can bake them in the coals."

"What are potatoes?"

"Vegetables."

"I don't think I'll like them."

"Don't start with me, William."

The simplicity of the phrase gave him pause, as he would like nothing better than to *start* with her. He'd begin by pulling that horsetail arrangement out of her hair.

"Why do you bind your hair so?"

"To keep it out of my eyes. It's always so breezy here."

"Not in the castle." He'd work his way down the back of her neck with light kisses, slip the wide scoop of her tunic off her shoulder and caress it tenderly...

"I'm outside a lot."

"I see." What he would like to see was her creamy bare skin, petal soft and flushed with his kisses.

"Besides..."

He couldn't hear her over the roar in his head as he imagined his face pressed to her chest, the heat of her skin, the pounding of her heart picking up speed as he took her breast into his mouth.

"William."

"Silence!" If she'd be quiet just a little longer...

"The potatoes are ready."

He hung his head, only to find she'd left the running water and was standing in front of him, her legs bare beneath what Chelsie had informed him were shorts. So close, he could reach out and touch her skin—if he wanted a black eye.

He lifted his gaze. "Yes, m'lady?"

She handed him the first lump of shiny, crinkled silver. "These probably should have been started sooner, but we'll have to make do. At least they're small."

He turned it over and over in his palm, examining it, discovering that the silver was actually a wrapping; the thinnest metal he'd ever touched. He glanced up at her, torn between which he wanted to study more— the woman, or what she'd handed him.

"It goes in the coals?"

She grinned, and he chose *her*.

"I thought you were a medieval man who knows these things."

"M'lady teases me?" He took the rest of the potatoes from her and, still marveling over wrapping vegetables in metal instead of putting them into a stew pot, pushed them deep into the coals.

When he turned back, she was gone. He had no difficulty remembering her grin. In fact, if he were to be sucked into another time right then and there, he would take her memory with him forever.

She stayed away until hunger pains—or the savory aroma of two steaming hot hares—drew her back. He held no illusion that 'twas his presence in the castle that put that smile on her face, though he wished it were so. Chelsie and the old man appeared as William placed a large platter of meat and potatoes in the center of the wood table.

"'Tis ready, m'lady." He dogged her heels to her chair, where she stole a glance at him over her shoulder and, with a determined press of her lips, promptly seated herself. He placed his hand over his heart. "M'lady, you wound me."

She poised her hand above her shoulder.

"What is this?"

"If you have to kiss *something,* my hand will do."

"Never, m'lady." He bent over her shoulder and grazed her cheek with his own until he felt her turn ever so slightly toward him. Then, and only then, did he kiss her cheek.

"Me, too, me, too," Chelsie chanted.

William rounded the corner of the table and kissed the top of her head with a loud smack that made her laugh.

The old man—around the next corner—stood stiffly, his hand resting on his gun. "I'm thinking you best not be touching me, boy," he drawled.

"As you wish." William quickly slipped into the chair the old man had intended to take, as 'twas directly across the short length of the table from Livvy. There he was able to extend his legs and graze her tiny feet with his, though he took the greatest care not to squash hers beneath the work boots he'd borrowed.

What surprised him most was that she didn't withdraw. She peeked at him from beneath lowered lashes. He was unable to read her guarded expression, but actions spoke louder than words. She was warming up to him.

"It tastes like chicken, Mom."

"Hmm? Oh, the rabbit. I mean the hare. Use your fork, honey."

"William isn't."

She sighed and withdrew her feet.

"My apologies, m'lady." William picked up his fork, though he was not rewarded immediately.

He watched in rapt silence as Livvy took a tiny bite of meat with her perfectly straight, white teeth. When the tip of her tongue darted out to lick a spot of grease from her bottom lip, he nearly forgot they weren't alone, nearly cleared the dishes with a sweep of his arm and showed her what else a table could be used for.

"Mmm, this is wonderful, William."

Instead he carefully followed everyone's example, from wiping his hands on the small square of cloth by his plate to unwrapping and seasoning his potato.

"What is this?" he asked.

"Foil," Livvy replied, then rolled her eyes as if she hadn't intended to answer any more of his questions, but had been caught off guard.

Her foot finally sought his and, as her bare toes skimmed his ankle, he carefully folded his foil into a tiny keepsake.

"Where are you from, William?"

"Yeah, where?" the old man echoed, though his query sounded more like a demand.

"Right here."

"You were born in the village?"

"No, m'lady. In this castle. My mother—"

"Cool!" Chelsie exclaimed. "Show me which room, and we can charge admission."

The old man shot to his feet, his chair falling over backward with a loud crack of wood on stone. "Go back where you belong!" he ordered William, once again, before he pivoted and deserted the kitchen.

"Grandpa," Livvy called after him, to no avail. "William, I'm sorry. I don't know what's gotten into him."

"Yeah, who is he this week?" Chelsie muttered.

Something about Livvy's grandfather made William uneasy. Something familiar. "Many pardons, m'lady," he said as he rose from the table. "I must follow him."

CHELSIE ATE IN SILENCE—for all of thirty seconds, which was about all Livvy expected.

"May I please be excused?"

Livvy was tempted to acquiesce, simply to reward uncommonly good manners, but she'd seen the look that had passed between her grandfather and William, and she didn't think they'd be discussing anything suitable for an eight-year-old. Gently she said, "Stay and finish your supper."

Chelsie's lower lip stuck out. She pushed pieces of roasted hare, baked potato and canned green beans around on her plate, but none of it found its way into her mouth. "I'm never allowed to do anything."

"I think they've got grown-up things to discuss." Though just what those were piqued Livvy's curiosity. Maybe *she* should follow.

"I'm never allowed to help."

Livvy set her cup down and patiently asked, "How would you like to help?"

"I know we need money."

"Let me worry about that." She'd had a lot of practice in the last few hours.

"But no, listen. If we had a tournament, we could charge entry fees and admission, and sell hot dogs and soda and souvenirs—"

"Hello-*o*." Livvy waved her hand in front of Chelsie's face to slow her down and get her attention. "We're from Illinois, remember?"

"Uh-huh. So?"

"So what do we know about tournaments?"

"Not us, Mom. William. He knows all about them." With unbridled excitement, she bounced up onto her knees in her chair, and even then she couldn't hold still. She talked with her whole body in motion. "And it'd be a great publicity gimmick for the bed-and-breakfast."

"How old are you?"

Chelsie laughed. "Eight."

"Are you sure?"

"Mo-om."

"Who taught you all this stuff?"

"Grandma. She showed me how to write up contracts, too."

"You're eight years old."

"So?"

Livvy sighed. "Well, I can see I'd better start saving now for your college education. At the rate you're going, I won't have very long."

"Then we can do it?" Her eyes were bright blue and dancing with anticipation.

Livvy hated to disappoint her, but she had to be realistic. "We don't have enough time, and William won't be around long enough." Though it was possible that a tournament might attract a long-term investor or two.

Disappointment, then determination, flashed across Chelsie's fine features. "He'd stay for this, I know he would."

"I'm sure he's the moving-on type." *Figures.*

"Then we should ask him."

"Chelsie—"

"If you're sure he won't stay, what could it hurt?"

Livvy narrowed her eyes. "You're going to law school, right?"

Chelsie laughed.

"On two conditions. We *ask*. Period. One time. No badgering, no whining, no begging, no pouting."

"Mo-om."

"And two, he stays away from the workers. No sword demonstrations, no questions, no touching anything electrical. And three—"

"You said two."

"—no hare's blood, witch's potions..."

Chelsie giggled.

"Yeah, see, I learned from Grandma, too. Deal?" She wasn't totally against the idea of William staying—after all, he *had* slain a couple of hares for her. They weren't dragons, but, hey, who knew when she'd find a real one of those lurking about?

He'd defended her castle by throwing Leo out the door. It wasn't an army by any means, but the intent was there. His armor wasn't shiny, but he'd stood up to her grandfather; something not many men would do.

She was sure he wouldn't stay. A man with an imagination like his had to be headed for a career somewhere else.

"Deal," Chelsie agreed. "I'll have it all worked out before I go to bed."

All in all, he wasn't Mr. Right—jeez, he'd nearly broken a leg jumping out of her bed—so what was the point in wanting him to stay?

THE OLD MAN, with amazing agility for his age, scurried through the castle's passageways and up three flights of stairs. While William couldn't keep him in sight the whole time, he never lost the sound of rapid footsteps on stone.

It occurred to William that Livvy's grandfather was baiting him and never intended to lose him. As they neared the study, a room which portended mystery and danger to William, he kept his hand on his sword. Just in case.

This was also the room in which he'd met the lovely Livvy, whom he wasn't ready to abandon just yet. If he couldn't stay in this time and have his castle back, he'd like for her to keep it. In spite of the horrendous changes she was making, it was better than Marsh Castle falling into the hands of that scoundrel, Leo.

So, if William could avoid any pitfalls and stay a little longer, that would be his wish. He eased himself through the doorway, into the study, with utmost caution.

The old man, standing by the window, turned slowly to greet him. "I told you to go back where you came from!"

"I've yet to figure out how I got here. Perhaps you can help me?"

The old man wrenched a sword off the wall. "I'll help you, all right."

William pasted on a smile he was far from feeling. "I was hoping you could answer a few questions."

"You won't have time to ask them." The old man lunged forward, thrusting his sword at William's midsection.

William drew his own sword in time to deflect metal with metal. "Your haste reminds me of someone."

"No kidding." The old man lunged again, forcing William to defend himself a second time.

"Someone foolish." A niggling of doubt, perhaps dread, crept up William's spine.

"Not so foolish."

As the old man lunged forward a third time, as the

clang of sword meeting sword rang out, William remembered having been in this position in this very room once before. He hadn't liked how it had ended then, and he wasn't about to do it again.

He didn't know which was to blame—the sword or the room—but there was only one he could change. He threw his sword down.

With glee, the old man swooped it up and disappeared. *Poof,* he was gone. Only his laughter lingered.

8

WILLIAM DIDN'T MOVE. He didn't dare.

"Edward?" he whispered, feeling the fool for thinking his brother and the old man could be one and the same. 'Twas not possible!

He feared that if he took one step in any direction, he'd be sucked along with the old man to another time. Forward again? The saints help him, no.

Back to his own time?

While that held merit, he was reluctant to leave Livvy to go to *any* other time. She surely didn't fit his requirements for a wife; she was far too sassy and opinionated—he grinned like a simpkin just thinking about her "unladylike" qualities—but he'd like to see her settled safely before he *had* to go.

He'd taken to thinking of her as the lovely Livvy. Never setting eyes on her again, never hearing her laugh, never watching her mother her child, never bantering with her—'twas all unacceptable.

Still, though, there was the possibility, and a knight who had lived to the ripe old age of thirty-five didn't get that way by ignoring possibilities. If he did go back to his own time, he'd like to know that some-where in the future, Livvy would live in his castle, sleep in his bed and maybe dream of him.

Because he knew, wherever and whenever he ended up, he'd be dreaming of her. Wishing he'd had more time to adjust to her ways. To her—the lovely Livvy. Most of all, wishing he could stay.

She hadn't believed that he'd traveled through time. How on earth was he going to tell her that her grandfather had just suffered the same fate?

Finally, when nothing happened, he dared to move his right foot, to test the floor in front of him. To one side, then the other. It seemed quite sound. He put his weight on that foot, took one step, then another.

He detected no changes. No black void. No feeling of being tossed out the window by a giant.

The door loomed ahead. He made his way there quickly, wanting to open it and see what was on the other side. Regular candles in the hall sconces, or the kind he'd chopped off?

Should he tell Livvy the truth, or make up some story to satisfy her? And for how long? It didn't seem he'd returned to his own time, so what were the odds her grandfather was coming back?

The code of chivalry he lived by was quite clear. He must be truthful—though he didn't necessarily have to volunteer the information, nor be prompt. The castle was large; maybe she wouldn't notice for a day or two that her grandfather was nowhere to be found.

First things first. He had to make his way to the armory and get another sword. No telling when he'd need one for self-defense or, if a villain were to suddenly appear out of nowhere, to protect Livvy.

With one last look over his shoulder, he pulled open the door, turned and saw the last person he wanted to see at that very moment: Livvy.

He nearly jumped out of his skin.

Arms folded across her chest, tapping her toe, she

was a study in impatience. "Well, I see you don't have any bullet holes in you."

"No, m'lady."

"Good." She brushed by him. "Grandpa, I heard you two talking, so I waited outside..."

From the doorway, William watched as she lapsed into silence and scanned the room.

"Where is he?"

"He...slipped out, m'lady."

"I was standing in the hall, William. I heard you arguing with him."

"Yes, m'lady." So much for delaying the inevitable. "We...uh, had a skirmish."

"So where is he?"

"Well, uh..." He scratched his head. "I don't know."

"You don't know?"

"He...disappeared, m'lady."

"Disappeared?" The arch of her eyebrows didn't fool him into thinking she was being swayed.

"Yes, m'lady." He decided to do the honorable thing, took a deep breath for fortitude and plunged ahead. "To another time, I fathom."

"Another time?"

"Yes, m'lady. 'Tis the very same manner in which I arrived here. I was in this room, dueling with my brother when, suddenly, *poof,* like a wisp of smoke, I was gone from there and landed here."

"*Poof?*"

"Aye, m'lady."

IN THREE SHORT MONTHS, Livvy had grown quite fond of her grandfather. She'd accepted his eccentric ways with a dose of humor, but that didn't mean she was ready, willing, or able to swallow the same line of B.S. from a total stranger. No matter how attractively it came packaged, William's story just didn't have the same effect on her.

And just when she'd begun to think she'd met a guy she could maybe like.

But she'd heard her grandfather and William in the study, arguing. There was only one door—that she knew of. And he was gone.

What was a woman to think? That it might be true? Because if it was, then William might really be an honest-to-Pete, old-fashioned knight.

Nah. There had to be a secret passage she hadn't discovered yet. He was forever going off on his own for days on end.

"I'll be in the kitchen cleaning up. If my grandfather comes back, will you tell him I'd like to talk to him?"

She was quite pleased with how calm she sounded. She hadn't called William a liar. She hadn't admitted that she was having second thoughts about him really coming from the fifteenth century.

She couldn't help it; she laughed.

"What, m'lady?"

"Oh, I was just considering—" She waved the thought away. "Nah, never mind. I'll be in the kitchen."

He dogged her heels. She didn't have to turn to see him; she could feel his eyes studying her backside through every hall, every room, down every flight of steps. Several times, he attempted to engage her in conversation.

"M'lady…"

She ignored him and kept on her way. In the

kitchen, she scooped dirty dishes off the table and carried them to the sink. She noticed William didn't help with the rest. Yeah, maybe he *was* from another century.

"M'lady, what are you doing?"

She continued scraping plates into the trash, in spite of William's appalled tone.

"M'lady, I beg you, 'tis proper to give that to the almoner."

She couldn't help herself, she looked up at him. "The who?"

"The almoner. 'Tis tradition for him to distribute what you don't want to the poor and needy."

He was either really good, really crazy, or really from another century.

Any of the above, and she was in trouble. If he was so concerned for others, she'd probably fall head over heels for him—a tragedy, considering he didn't want her. If he was crazy, she didn't need him in her life; she had a child to protect. And if he was from another time, she was in way over her head.

Tonight, when she went to bed, she was going to lock her door, and she'd have Chelsie with her. Just in case.

"WE'RE GONNA HAVE a tournament," Chelsie informed William that evening. "My mom says so."

"Is that right?"

"Uh-huh. Before the end of the month."

"And how long is that?"

"Two weeks. A fortnight in your time."

William laughed. "'Tis impossible. Why, the messengers couldn't cover enough ground in that time."

Though, if they could... He remembered the speed with which the trucks moved.

"I'll get on the Internet."

"'Tis faster than horses?"

"It's faster than trucks."

Impossible! "'Twill bring many men?"

"Sure."

"Unwed men?"

She shrugged, but it didn't matter. William knew a tournament would bring him scores of men from which to choose a husband for Livvy.

"I shall think on it."

"We'll split it sixty/forty."

WILLIAM HOVERED at the foot of the bed—the same one he'd slept in five hundred years ago. It had felt different when he'd crawled into it the last time; definitely not stuffed with straw or feathers; definitely more luxurious. These twentieth-century people sure knew how to live, in spite of the fact that they'd done away with much that was good, too.

He backed off a step when Livvy sighed in her sleep and rolled over, turning her back to Chelsie, who was sprawled out as if the whole bed were hers. When neither of them wakened, he stepped closer again.

Livvy's hair was loose, the way he'd wanted to see it, cascading over her pillow and shoulders, begging to be stroked. In spite of the chill in the room, the blanket dipped low, revealing the thin strap that held on her gown.

Difficult as 'twas to leave her side, and praising his foresight, he stepped away just long enough to light the fire he'd carefully laid for her hours ago. As it caught, he unfolded the foil he'd saved, then experimented with it, refolding it into a crude heart, amazed that he could smooth it out and try again. With practice, he'd do better. Just like with Livvy.

He strolled back to her bedside, filled his lungs with the scent he now associated with Livvy, and Livvy alone. He must remember to ask her its name. First thing in the morning, if he was still here. In the meantime, he must watch over her and keep her safe.

If traveling through time was possible—and he knew 'twas—was it just he and Edward and her grandfather who were able to do it? Or could anyone appear at anytime, once they knew the magic? Or once they were cursed?

Did it have something to do with the study? The swords? If 'twas the swords, they were both in another time now. Maybe with her grandfather; maybe in different times.

Too many questions! No answers.

Faced with the realization that he, too, could be sucked away at any moment, William knew he couldn't agree to help Chelsie with the tournament. In order to avoid her tears, he must get her to decide against it for herself, though she was a most headstrong child. Like her mother.

He would find Livvy a husband another way.

Pain sliced through his heart at the thought of her with another man. He identified it as jealousy, then pushed all such thoughts aside. 'Twas for her own good.

If another man were to travel through time and appear in Marsh Castle, William wanted to be ready to defend it and Livvy. He needed another sword—now. With one last long, lingering look at her, he returned to the secret passage, closed the door silently behind him and hoped the armory hadn't fallen victim to Livvy's rebuilding.

FOR DAYS, Livvy helped Chelsie plan the tournament while William unexpectedly threw up roadblocks.

"There isn't much time to prepare," he said once.

"Then let's get busy," Livvy argued.

"Yeah," Chelsie added.

Another time he said, "I don't know...are tournaments still popular?"

"Maybe people are starving for this kind of entertainment." She worried that if he didn't get behind this, there'd be no chance at all.

"Yeah, c'mon, William," Chelsie added.

He procrastinated until the electricity was fixed. The workers resumed renovations. Sarah returned. Chelsie got on the Internet and sent out bulletins about the tournament.

"Okay, we're committed now," Livvy pronounced at supper one evening.

"You're very headstrong, m'lady."

"I like to get things done, if that's what you mean."

"You like to change things."

She grinned, remembering her father, a civil engineer who had dragged her all over the country from one project to another. "It's in my genes."

If only her roots were as easy to trace. As soon as the tournament was over, after the bed-and-breakfast was open—she refused to think *if* it opened—she'd resume the search. Surely the line had to go farther back than her grandfather. It just wasn't possible that there was no record of his birth anywhere.

"Chelsie," William said, "wouldn't you rather search through the castle for secret passages than sit out in the sun and watch knights play at war games?"

"Nope."

"'Twill make your freckles worse."

As Chelsie's brows dipped into a frown and her lower lip jutted out, Livvy shot a warning glance at William. Too late, she realized, as tears slid silently down her daughter's cheeks and dripped onto her plate. Her lower lip trembled.

"My mom needs money to pay Leo back so we can stay here."

"Can you possibly make enough?" he asked, his tone laced heavily with doubt. Not concern, but doubt.

"Maybe not," Livvy answered, "but I'm hoping to attract another creditor who will buy the note from Leo. And why do you persist in making this difficult when you were so eager before?" She, also, lost her appetite.

"Yeah," Chelsie shouted, and didn't even attempt to hide her tears.

"There, there," William murmured.

Livvy watched in awe as he reached out and patted her daughter's shoulder tenderly, then remembered he'd said he'd had a little girl once. She hadn't believed him, of course, because she hadn't believed anything he'd said, but now she wondered if maybe this one tiny part was true.

"A tournament is not a game for females to concern themselves with," he said softly. "You are only supposed to sit and watch and applaud your knight."

He drew Chelsie out of her chair and onto his lap,

and Livvy had to stifle the urge to trade places with her.

Looking much like a man caught between a rock and a hard place, he glanced at Livvy. "And maybe grant your favorite knight the honor of wearing your scarf."

She'd tear her drawers apart until she found one.

"I'm just trying to protect you both."

"We don't need your protection, William. You seem to know a lot about knights and chivalry and weapons. We need your expertise."

He dipped his head in the slightest of bows. "As m'lady wishes."

Chelsie's head rested comfortably beneath his chin, and a warmth had entered his eyes that Livvy hadn't seen before. With a little imagination, he really could be her knight in shining armor—even if it was tarnished.

WILLIAM'S HEAD was spinning, and it had nothing to do with flying through time. Not exactly.

Something about the old man had bothered William since the morning he'd ridden into the knights' camp and bellowed at William to leave, to go back where he came from. Had the old man somehow known that William didn't belong in this time?

Then, when William had entered the study and seen him by the window, when he'd come at William with a sword, ready to do battle, 'twas a sense of déjà vu. It had happened before. Five hundred years ago.

He needed confirmation, though.

He found Livvy sitting in a smaller, more modern version of his father's study. She was behind a desk, as if she'd been working, but, sprawled in the chair with her feet up on a drawer, he doubted it.

"M'lady..."

"Hmm?" Slowly she rose to a more decorous position.

"Might I ask you a question about your grandfather?"

She rolled her eyes in that fashion of which he'd become quite enamored.

"Yes," she said, "he's peculiar. We all know it, so there, I said it out loud."

"Peculiar?" 'Twas not what he was going to ask about, but it might tell him more.

"What can I say? He's fixated on the Wild West."

"Wild West?"

"William," she said on a sigh, "give it a rest, would you?"

Chelsie, whom he hadn't seen perched on the edge of the bow window, answered. "The American Wild West. They had cowboys and Indians and stagecoaches and six-shooters and buffalo—"

William held up both hands to stop her rattling off anything else he'd never heard of before. "None of this helps." At her crestfallen look, he quickly added, "Though I appreciate your effort. Perhaps we can go into all that later."

Chelsie shrugged good-naturedly.

"Now, m'lady, if I might ask... What is your grandfather's name?"

"Edward Marsh, as if you didn't kno—"

"No!"

She jumped—nearly out of her chair.

'Twas the answer he'd expected, yet it couldn't be! "You are certain?"

"Hey, I've been working on this in my spare time for over a year. I've asked my mom, I've done the libraries, the genealogical societies, the bibles, the churches. If there's one thing I'm certain of, it's—"

"Silence! M'lady, you are just like your child. I asked only if you are certain that he is Edward."

She wrinkled her nose at him, something no woman in his time would have done. At least not to his face, unless they wanted to bear the sharp edge of his tongue.

"Yes, I'm sure."

He could no longer wonder whether the old man was his younger brother, Edward. He was sure of it. What he wasn't sure of was how he was now an old man. If there were rules about traveling through time, William sure didn't know what they were. Apparently, they'd landed in two different times. Apparently Edward had gotten here first, retaken the castle and had a family.

And just as apparently, Livvy was William's blood relative—his own brother's granddaughter.

Now he not only had to find her a husband to protect her, but he also had to find one who would take her far, far away, so he wouldn't have to see her every day and lust after forbidden fruit.

"Is that all?"

"Is that all?" he boomed. "Isn't it enough?"

THE DAYS BEFORE the tournament passed quickly. William oversaw the carpenters as he had them build stands for spectators. And Livvy had to oversee him, as he tried to build what he called a berfrois.

"What's that?" she asked.

"A stand for the ladies."

"William, no one's convinced me of time travel yet, so I'm going to have to assume you are either suffering from a weird amnesia or you're demented."

"I am neither, m'lady. But what does this have to do with the berfrois?"

"Women don't sit separate from men."

"Ah," he said with apparent glee, "if you've never been to a tournament, how do you know this?"

Her response could only be described as a frustrated scream in the back of her throat. "Fine. Build it, but don't be surprised when it's taken over by anyone with a ticket."

He built a quintain, a pole with a cross beam holding a sack of sand on one end, a shield from the armory on the other. Then, with his gold spurs now worn on his work boots, he mounted Silver, tucked a lance in place, charged the shield and demonstrated how a knight had to quickly get out of the way before the sack of sand spun around and hit him in the back.

"I want to try it!" Chelsie squealed.

"Get in line," Livvy said.

"M'lady, no!"

"And why not?" Livvy and Chelsie both asked together, just as they both fisted their hands on their hips.

Knowing she was Edward's granddaughter, he snapped his gaze up above her chin. "'Tis not proper."

"Oh, pshaw. Get down off that horse."

"Over my dead body." He turned Silver and rode away.

Livvy let him get a hundred feet, put her fingers between her teeth and blew a quick, shrill whistle, to which Silver had been trained to respond. William, though, exhibited horsemanship skills that would have earned him his knighthood—*if* this were the Middle Ages. Silver fought the aids, but, in the end, carried William off to the stables.

"Men!" Chelsie said, with a shake of her head, before Livvy could.

THE NIGHT BEFORE the tournament, after Livvy had her last meeting with the villagers who had agreed to run concessions the next day, she went to tuck Chelsie in for the night. Usually they had a playful tug-of-war over the pencil and notebook. Only after that was Chelsie exhausted and relaxed enough to drift off to sleep.

Tonight Livvy found William sitting on Chelsie's bed, leaning against the headboard, his boots and spurs hanging off the edge of the mattress. Chelsie, tucked beneath his arm, her head pillowed on his broad chest, her eyes at half-mast, listened to him tell a story.

"...So King Arthur sent for Guinevere to be his bride," William related in a soft, masculine tone.

Chelsie yawned. "What about Lancelot?"

"You know of this story?"

She nodded. "My grandpa told me."

"Ah. Well, then, you know you must wait a bit for that part."

Livvy leaned against the cool, stone wall in the hallway, closed her eyes and listened to William's smooth, deep cadence as he told his own version of the story, using words which Chelsie sometimes made him stop and clarify; old words which crept into her grandfather's speech at odd moments.

Loony or not, from this century or not, Livvy liked

William. She supposed her easy acceptance of him had something to do with living with her grandfather for three months and growing accustomed to eccentricity.

Listening to William's deep murmurs on the other side of the wall, she experienced a pang of loneliness, the kind a woman feels when she's been without a man too long and is cramped up in a castle with one to die for.

Okay, cramped might be an exaggeration. All the same, he'd been in her bed once. If he hadn't fled from it, she'd have kicked him out. Then.

Perhaps not now.

For the past several days, he'd kept his distance from her, she was certain of it. No long, lingering looks. No bumping her knees under the kitchen table.

If he continued to withdraw, she couldn't count on him making another pass at her, one she could follow up on.

She'd never been shy before. She'd take matters into her own hands, if she could just track him down and get him to hold still for more than a minute.

Tomorrow was the tournament. He'd be distracted; a perfect opportunity.

9

_____

BY THE SAINTS! The world had gone mad.

William barely slept the night before the tournament, which had little to do with the fact that only two knights—unfortunately, they were already wed—had shown up so far. Knights normally traveled long distances to tournaments and would often camp for days ahead of time.

Nor did it have anything to do with the way *they* carted their *horses,* instead of the other way around, pulling them in wagons hitched behind trucks. Although that was enough to keep any God-fearing knight on his toes.

Instead his restlessness had everything to do with sleeping with no more than one wall between him and Livvy.

For days, he'd worked sunup to sundown in order to keep his mind off her. He'd paced off the tournament list and built the tilt barrier.

He'd fitted his lance with prongs, rehabbed an old saddle—there was no way he'd be safe on Edward's—searched high and low until he found armor to fit the horse.

He'd built stands for minstrels and spectators. After a long search through the village, he'd found a young man who agreed to serve as his squire.

And yet, with all that and more, he lay awake and

thought about Livvy until he could stand it no more. Long before dawn, he rose, dressed in his own clothes—the ones in which he'd arrived—and ran outdoors to the tournament list until his heart pounded fiercely and his breath was labored.

He fell onto bended knee and prayed for just one decent, unwed knight to arrive, one who would marry Livvy and take her far, far away.

His prayer was answered a hundredfold, it seemed, as truck after truck pulled onto the castle grounds soon after dawn, all pulling horse trailers.

Ah, well, he'd take them any way he could get them.

A driver leaned out his open window. "Hey, where do I park?"

"Are ye wed?"

"No." He lifted his cap and scratched his head. "But what's that got to do with—"

William grinned and pointed off to the left. "You may *park* yonder."

He had no idea why every truck paused by him, but, since they did, he stood his ground and divided them according to marital status, grinning all the while. This would make his search so much simpler. He could wander about, picking and choosing prospective husbands as he went, without concern about weeding the unwed men out again.

"How's it going?" Livvy asked when she arrived at his side.

"Wonderful, m'lady." He waved yet another unwed prospect off to the left. "Just wonder— What the hell are you wearing?"

"What's it look like?"

Had the woman no sense at all?

She pirouetted gaily in, of all things, breeches. And not just any plain old pair, but one the color of the sun. Her long tunic was randomly studded with tiny jewels.

"It looks like a tent."

"It's a maternity outfit. I couldn't fit in any of my old skirts, and the spandex shorts didn't seem appropriate for today."

"But you're...you're..."

"Showing?" She smiled and batted her eyes as if that were a *good* thing.

"Yes! What man will even take a second look at you now?"

Her laugh was as light as the breeze fluttering through the wispy tendrils curled along her neck. "I've seen you looking."

"Impossible! You were asleep." As soon as the words passed his lips, he knew he'd made a big mistake.

Her smile faltered. "You were in my room?"

He turned to the next driver. "Are ye wed?"

"Yeah, but what's that got to do with—"

"Park yonder." He waved him to the right.

Livvy grabbed his doublet sleeve and held firm until he gave in and faced her. "Were you in my room last night?"

"Aye, m'lady." He saw no need to volunteer that he'd checked in on her every night, especially since the door was locked on more than one occasion.

"And the night I had a fire? *You* lit it, didn't you? Not Chelsie."

"Hey, bud, where do I park this rig?"

Grateful for the distraction, William turned to answer the driver.

Livvy made tracks in the other direction, knowing she had to apologize to Chelsie for lecturing her about using matches unsupervised. Other than that, Chelsie wasn't the one on her mind now.

If William had climbed into bed with her again, she'd have welcomed him, but it was apparent that he had some hang-up about her carrying another man's child. Somehow, she had to let him know that she was willing without coming right out and dragging him off to bed by his hair.

Although, that idea had merit.

WILLIAM KEPT A WATCHFUL eye on every knight at the tournament, and over a hundred had entered. Many of the wed knights had unwed sons with them. Some were a bit younger than Livvy and probably didn't have the experience necessary to handle her sassy tongue, but, as far as William was concerned, they were still fair game.

"There, that one." With a tilt of his head, he pointed out a particularly good-looking prospect for Chelsie, seated beside him in the front row of the stands, to look over.

"Mmm." She drew out the hum as she puckered her brow, rested her chin on her fist and appeared to give his choice the consideration it deserved. "Nope."

"But he's fine-looking and strong."

"He's a dweeb."

"What is this word, *dweeb?*"

She wrinkled her nose and shrugged. "He just is."

"Dweebs don't make good husbands?"

She shrugged, as if the question weren't important enough to bother with an answer.

Knights lined up to run the rings without their helms—there was no danger involved in galloping their steeds down the field and attempting to pluck a ring off a horizontal pole with their lance—and he scanned them one and all.

"There, that one. Third in line."

"Too short."

"Fourth, then."

"Too old."

"Your mother needs someone older. Someone who will keep her in line."

Chelsie giggled.

"What?"

She giggled harder, and he didn't think it dignified to pursue the matter in public.

Four knights paired up for a demonstration of the tilt. Their great helms went on, making it difficult for William to continue, as he had to match coats of arms with unwed men he'd seen for the first time that morning.

He thought both men in the first pair were wed, so, after briefly assessing their skills for when he would compete against them later, he turned his attention to the second pair as they galloped along the tilt barrier toward each other.

"There, the far one is unwed. He sits his horse well."

His selection hit the ground headfirst.

"Not as well as you," Chelsie said with a wicked smile.

He growled his frustration. "You're very much like your mother. Why is that truck on my field?"

As he rose, Chelsie grabbed his hand and tugged on his arm.

"I must order them off."

"It's an ambulance, and those men take care of people who get hurt." She tugged until he reseated himself. "Is this dangerous?"

"Indeed."

"I thought it was just supposed to be fun."

"Aye, 'tis, but there's an element of danger in any game of war." William rose again, rubbing his hands together in anticipation of his turn.

"Where are you going?" Chelsie asked anxiously.

"'Tis time for me to get ready for my event."

"B-but I thought we were going to pick out a man for my mom."

"As you wish." He searched one out. "That one."

"Uh...no."

He pointed toward another. "That one?"

"Um, nope."

He selected another without even looking. "Him?"

"Nope."

He raked his fingers through his hair. "You pick one, then."

She looked up at him with a plea in her eyes. "You."

FOR HOURS, Livvy tapped all likely sources of revenue—everyone who had arrived in an expensive car, dripped in diamonds, or looked to have two extra cents to their name. None seemed promising.

She had many other things to occupy her mind, none of which did for very long. Concessions, for one thing, could use some watching. Or her grandfather, who might decide to make an appearance and take this opportunity to show off his skills with a lasso or six-shooter, even though they weren't a scheduled event.

What *did* occupy her mind was a certain dashing knight in shining armor. William had finally cleaned his suit from head to toe. It appeared he'd even banged out a couple of dents.

Mounted on Silver, who was draped in a flowing royal blue fabric that looked suspiciously like new curtains from one of the guest rooms, William could be the genuine article—if such a thing were possible.

Was it? Sometimes she was tempted to think so, because he *never* slipped up. And her grandfather *had* disappeared from a room while she stood outside the door.

"Oh, sorry," she murmured an apology for bumping into someone, but couldn't tear her gaze from William as he turned Silver toward her.

"M'lady."

His helmet was tucked beneath his arm, allowing her to feast her eyes on his thick black hair, steel gray eyes and strong jaw. The tiny scar beside his left eye spoke of past injury, and she wondered if he'd gotten it playing at being a knight. Or really *being* a knight.

Nah.

And she remembered other scars, ones she was hoping to see again sometime soon. All six of them. Maybe more.

"You'll be careful?" she asked.

"Aye, m'lady. You needn't worry about me."

"Oh, I'm not worried," she lied. "I just don't have any bandages handy."

"'Tis custom for the lady of the castle to choose a knight to champion her."

"Really?" She surveyed the mounted knights. "Do you have anyone in mind?"

"Several, m'lady. But only one can wear your scarf."

"Well, then." She sighed as if it were a major decision. "I guess it'll have to be you."

"'Twould be an honor, m'lady, but—"

"You're turning me down?"

"Uh…"

"It wouldn't be a very chivalrous thing to do, William."

He blinked. "I would be honored, m'lady."

She stood on the bottom seat of the stands and slowly reached up to pat the red scrunchy holding her hair. "I couldn't find a scarf. Will this ol' thing do?"

"Aye."

Tugging gently, she let it slide from her hair, inch by inch, making him wait for it. She was new at the game of intentionally being provocative, but, from the sudden gleam in his eyes, she assumed she was on the right track. She dangled the scrunchy just out of his reach, tempting him closer.

After dismounting Silver with great ease, he approached her. The moment his fingers touched hers, she stood up from the bleachers and moved closer. Planting her hand on the vambrace which protected his arm, she lifted up on tiptoe, aiming a kiss for luck toward his smooth cheek.

His other hand shot out and landed on her shoulder before she could make contact. He pushed her back. Gently but definitely. Almost as if he were protecting her. From him?

Okay, she'd try harder.

By LATE AFTERNOON, Livvy couldn't believe her grandfather still hadn't shown up from wherever he'd gone. She knew he'd left from the study, and it was there she went in search of a secret door. If she could discover which way he'd gone, maybe she'd find out what happened to him.

Slowly she made her way around the entire perimeter of the room, knocking on paneling, tugging at arms on statues to see if they twisted, pushing knotholes to see if they were secret buttons. Nothing happened, of course.

Not that I thought it would.

She seated herself behind the desk and rifled through the drawers. The only interesting thing she found was a rolled-up canvas, an oil painting of her grandfather dressed as a cowboy sheriff. That part didn't surprise her too much. Next to him was an Indian woman, her hair laced in a long, gray braid, her doeskin dress adorned with beads that matched her necklace.

So, she'd gained nothing by searching. She bent down and stuck the rerolled canvas back into the empty drawer.

There, her head practically beneath the desk, she could see the floor in front of it. And right there, a pair of feet, encased in her grandfather's black cowboy boots, landed.

Actually *landed.*

She shot to her feet to find him in the flesh, a sword in each hand, cackling like a fool.

"*Whoo-ee!* I'm gettin' that landin' down pretty good." He sheathed one sword across his chest and slapped his thigh.

She must have squeaked, because he pivoted around and looked as shocked as she felt.

"Livvy, girl! I'm back." Excited, as charged up as a little boy in a roomful of Christmas presents, he rushed around the desk, sheathed a second sword behind his back and grasped her by the arms. "Did you see me, Livvy?"

She tipped her head up and studied the ceiling, hoping to find a big, gaping hole in it.

No such luck.

"Did you see me land?"

She felt her head nod, though she was certain she didn't have the power to tell it to do so. As soon as he released her, her rear hit the chair with a thud.

"Grandpa…"

He rubbed his hands together. "It works, I tell you! It works." He ran out the door, calling "William!" as he went.

Livvy pinched herself on the arm, and it hurt like the dickens.

"Oh my God, he's not crazy." And it wasn't her grandfather she was thinking about.

It was William, who swore he was lord of Marsh Castle. He hadn't slipped up, all right—not because he was really good, but because he was *real*.

And she'd doubted him.

She made tracks for the tournament field. Instead of finding him with Chelsie—they'd had their heads together practically all day—she found him in a heated debate with Leo.

"Well, well, well." Leo wore a coat of mail, a sword at his side and a brightly painted shield on one arm.

She tugged on William's arm impatiently. "I need you."

It was a Freudian slip, she supposed. She should have said she needed to talk to him, but she really did need him. He was honest and real. He was patient with her daughter. When he looked at Livvy, he made her feel like the only woman in the world.

"First, m'lady, I must deal with this insolent heathen."

Leo's laugh was wicked. "I was just telling your friend here, Mrs. Ravenwood, that the tournament is a nice try, but in spite of all this—"

Leo's manner, as he observed the knights and spectators, and then her, was patronizing, at the very least.

"—Marsh Castle will soon be mine."

She wanted to slap the man, started to, but William's fingers grazed her arm, and she didn't want to move.

Leo continued, "I could, say, *arrange* to keep you on, little lady." He winked. "If you know what I mean."

Enough was enough. She drew her arm back to get up enough speed for a good, sound whack, which she never got the pleasure of delivering because William caught her wrist. While the two men did their macho-stud dance, she tested William's grasp to find it as secure as a manacle.

"Marsh Castle will never belong to a Leopold," he challenged.

Leo's expression was a mixture of surprise and intrigue. "Say, how did you know—?"

"Prepare to defend yourself, unless you are the coward I think you are."

Leo's laugh shook his rotund belly. In answer, he

patted his own sword and raised his shield. "I can't wait."

"Now hold on just a minute," Livvy scolded, but, by that time, Leo had stalked away and William was already giving her orders.

"Stay in the stands, m'lady. You'll be safe there."

"You are *not* going to duel with him, William."

"I can defeat the likes of him with one hand tied behind my back."

"That's not the point. Whether you win or not, he still gets the castle if I can't pay off the note."

"When I win, I'll hold him for ransom. He must pay for his release. 'Tis the code."

"He doesn't live by any code," she said scathingly, wondering whether they were fighting over the castle or over her.

Isn't this what she'd thought would be romantic?

I must have been nuts.

"But I do, m'lady, and he will honor it. Or else I'll cut out his—"

"No! I don't want you to cut out anything. I forbid you to cut out anything. Oh, God, is this what you men used to be like?"

William's eyebrows arched with obvious humor. "You forbid me, m'lady?"

She took a deep breath and squared her shoulders. If this is what it took to keep him from getting hurt...

"Yes, I do."

"I am lord of this castle," he boomed, his arm swinging around and encompassing all that she and her grandfather owned.

"Yes, I know. I do, William, I know. I believe you, I swear."

"*You* will obey *me*."

"In your dreams," she said haughtily.

Amazingly his cheeks blazed red. And he was speechless for a change. He pivoted and clattered off toward the field, handing his helmet and Silver off to his squire as he did so.

He barked orders, and space was cleared for Leo and him. They drew their swords, only to have a tournament official order them both off the field for unfair play with unblunted tips.

They shoved him out of their way.

"Cool," Chelsie said as she wandered over, pretzel in hand. "Want some?"

"Huh? Oh, no thanks." Livvy barely glanced at her daughter, but allowed her to lead her a few yards to the first bleacher.

"Sit down, Mom."

She shook her head as Leo lunged at William with his sword.

"You're blocking the people behind you, Mom."

"Oh." She sat—for all of three seconds—then she was back on her feet, her fingers clenched into fists.

It was soon evident that, compared to William, Leo must have learned sword fighting from some learn-in-the-privacy-of-your-own-home video. Moments later, his weapon flew out of his hand. He dived for it and, for his trouble, ended up in the dirt with William's foot on his wrist and the tip of the blade at his throat.

"Do ye pledge?"

"What?" He tried to swallow, but it looked uncomfortable. "Hell no!"

Livvy winced as the tip poked deeper into Leo's skin.

"Make the pledge."

"What pledge?"

"Would you have me disembowel you right here?"

Livvy slumped onto the bleacher seat.

"Pledge that you'll remain on my land until your ransom is paid."

"How...how much?"

William glanced at Livvy. "However much m'lady has borrowed on Marsh Castle."

"Never!"

Livvy covered her eyes. She'd finally found a knight in shining armor and, if he wasn't whisked away into yet another century, he was surely headed for prison.

10

WITH HIS BLADE to Leo's throat, William's intent was to get Livvy out of debt to the scoundrel, not kill him in front of women and children. He sheathed his sword, pulled his poleax from his belt and grabbed Leo by the ear.

"Someone bring me a nail," he bellowed.

Gripping Leo by his earlobe, William dragged him toward the stands. He didn't have a proper pole to nail the man to, but any wood would do, as long as 'twould hold.

The loud crack of a gunshot split the heavy silence. Knights, spectators and officials scattered in all directions as if they were leaves on the wind.

"Grandpa!" Chelsie sprinted from the bleachers and wrapped her arms around the old man's waist.

Edward held his gun in the air and fired yet another shot.

From the same weapon?

"How can this be?" William demanded, astonished by the gun's capabilities.

If he had to fight Edward for the castle again, 'twould be difficult to win against such odds. Not that William minded the challenge, but Livvy needed his protection until he settled her with a husband. He'd be able to safeguard her well with a gun that didn't need reloading.

Edward lowered his spectacular weapon. "Put down your sword, William."

"Not for any man."

Leo took full advantage of their exchange and slipped out of William's grasp. Covered with dust, he still had the audacity to make threats as he slunk off.

"'Twould be a mistake to leave my lands," William warned him, though he kept an eye on Edward as he did so.

He was dressed differently than when he'd disappeared from the study. Now he wore a vest of smooth leather with a silver star over his heart. His belt had a pocket for a gun on each hip, though the one on his left wasn't in very good condition with all those notches on the handle. A sword hung across his chest. The one strung across Edward's back, William assumed was his.

"'Tis kind of you to return my sword."

"We have unfinished business."

"'Tis my castle, Edward, and I'll fight any man who says otherwise."

EVERY MAN LIVVY HAD MET in the last three months had been scared of her grandfather's unpredictable nature—except William.

It was just her luck she'd have to choose between a grandfather, who lived like a throwback to the American Wild West, and a man who believed—no, *was* a knight from the Middle Ages.

What was a woman to do?

While she was sure she loved her grandfather, she wasn't so sure she'd use that same word about William. Especially at the moment, when he was making the term *unpredictable* seem rather tame.

Other than William, Edward and Chelsie, Livvy was the only person left standing out in the open. She covered the ground between them quickly.

"Chelsie, get back." While Livvy didn't believe either man would hurt her, they had three swords, a pair of pistols and unfinished business between them.

"But, Mo-om—"

She unwrapped her daughter's arms from around her grandfather. "Go. I don't have time to argue with you."

The spectators and knights gradually eased forward, circling them, but William glared at Edward as if they were still alone on the field. Somehow, she had to find a compromise both men could live with, as she sensed neither of them would back down. Ever.

Half of Marsh Castle was hers. Maybe…just maybe…she could share her half ownership with William. That seemed fair. After all, it had been in her family now for ages. She'd make the offer, but only if he agreed not to fight with her grandfather or have his way with Leo's intestines.

Is this what women went through in the Middle Ages? Did they have to worry about their men constantly killing each other off to prove they were better or stronger or owned property coveted by another?

If so, she took back every fantasy she'd ever had about knights.

Taking a deep breath, she steeled herself for what was to come. "Okay, fellas—" she turned toward them "—put down those weapons and… What the hell are you doing?"

William, the taller of the two, had his arms draped over Edward's shoulders as he hugged him to his chest. Edward embraced him, also, and they were slapping each other on the back and laughing like a pair of fools.

"Never mind," her grandfather said heartily. "It's your castle, William, and welcome to it."

Livvy blinked. She smacked the heel of her hand against her ear so she could hear what he was *really* saying.

"I don't need it anyway," he added.

"Well, wait just a minute," Livvy objected, but they didn't seem to notice.

"Where did you go?" William asked him.

"I didn't go *where* I wanted—the swords don't work that way—but it was the right time. That's why I don't need the castle anymore."

"Well, I do!" Livvy interjected. When they still ignored her, she stomped across the trampled grass and wiggled herself between them. "It's one thing to share, Grandpa, but you can't just give away my half. Why, that's like…like some feudal lord or something."

EDWARD.

This was the brother William remembered from his youth, the brother whose eyes had watered when William's wife and daughter were buried, and when William had saddled his horse and ridden away from Marsh Castle.

He sidestepped Livvy and held the old man at arm's length, mirroring his grin. "'Tis good to finally laugh with you again."

"Aye. Me, too, William."

"Excuse me…" Livvy said.

William yanked on Edward's gray hair. "You haven't aged well, though, brother."

Livvy's head pivoted. "Brother?"

"Aye, this old man is my younger brother," William boasted.

"Uh, William, I wouldn't say that too loud," she whispered.

William, happy only to have his brother back, didn't care who knew there were peculiar circumstances involved. "Why not?"

"Because people who don't understand will send men for you. Men with white jackets that buckle in the back."

"It sounds like a most odd garment," he mused.

"We're not crazy, Livvy," Edward said.

"I'm glad we're of a same mind now, Edward," William said heartily.

"The same mind—I *knew* there was something about you two that worried me."

"Livvy…"

"Other than you—" she wheeled on Edward "—trying to give away my half of the castle."

William was fascinated to watch Livvy chastise his brother. Women didn't speak this way to men, especially their elders. Why, in his time, Edward would have every right to beat her and lock her in the tower, though he didn't seem inclined to do so now.

"We have an agreement," she continued, shoving her way between them again, waggling her finger under Edward's nose. "*I* get the loan, *I* do the work, *you* give me half the castle. Sound familiar?"

"Now, Livvy girl—" Edward said soothingly.

"If not, I have it in writing. I was thinking of sharing it with William, but—"

"Silence!"

Livvy wheeled on him, fire in her eyes that spoke

of a passion the likes of which he'd never experienced in a woman. Sharing sounded nice, were she not his brother's granddaughter.

"'Twould be my right to share with you, not the other way around, m'lady. The castle wasn't Edward's to give away."

Edward cleared his throat, which gained William's attention only because he was still overjoyed to be in the same era with his brother again—and to recognize him. If not for that, 'twould be quite difficult to take his mind off Livvy's fiery spirit at this point.

"Uh…William…maybe it wasn't mine five hundred years ago—"

"Definitely not."

"Yeah, definitely not," Edward agreed. "But it *was* mine to give away three months ago."

"Three months ago, 'twas still mine."

"Yeah, three months ago *then,* but not three months ago *now.* If you get my drift."

"No matter. I've arranged a suitable husband for Livvy. She'll be leaving on the morrow." He had more important matters on his mind, powerful matters that made him lower his voice to keep them secret. "As soon as she's settled, I'll be free to return home. You say 'tis the swords that have the magic?"

"YOU'VE ARRANGED…*WHAT?*" Livvy was sure her jaw dropped to her toes.

"A suitable husband, m'lady."

"You don't want me?" The question slipped out before she could bite back the words.

"M'lady!" *Appalled* would be too tame a description for his tone.

She didn't know whether to be more upset because

he didn't want her, or because the tyrant had arranged a "suitable" husband for her. Either way, he had to go. All she had to do was find a way to send the big lug packing before he embarrassed her to death.

She held her hand out, palm up. "I want my scrunchy back."

His dark brows puckered together. "What word is this, *scrunchy?*"

She grabbed the red fabric with both her hands and yanked it down off his arm. It snagged on his armor, but a little thing like that didn't stop her.

"William, I must tell you something," Edward said.

William held up his hand. "No need to thank me, brother. It has been my honor to solve this problem."

"Problem?" Livvy repeated through tight lips.

Edward took two steps back, William noted. If he were not lord of the castle, he might consider doing the same himself as Livvy advanced on him.

"Of all the outdated—"

William sighed. "M'lady, I have already explained this to you."

"—antiquated—"

"You need protection."

"—feudal—"

"You need a man."

She stepped forward until her breasts nearly touched his breastplate, and he chastised himself for thinking of her body in such terms.

"What about you?" she asked.

"Me? Oh, no, m'lady. 'Twould be wrong."

Edward said, "Uh, William..."

"Are you married?" she asked.

"No."

"Gay?"

"I am quite happy, but what's that got to do with—"

She fisted her hands on her hips. "Then why *'twould* it be wrong?"

Edward persisted. "Listen, William…"

"M'lady makes fun of me."

"*M'lady* wants to know what you're scared of, *Lord* William."

"Uh, there's something I ought to tell you both…"

She rested one hand on his breastplate in a provocative fashion.

"M'lady, no. 'Tis not right. I am your uncle."

Her fingers quit roaming over his armor—something he shouldn't be able to feel, but swore he could. Her lips froze with unspoken words on them. Confusion clouded her eyes momentarily.

Suddenly she shot backward, nearly tripping, landing smack up against Edward who said, "No, it's not true. Let me explain…"

She murmured, "But if you're really from the fifteenth—"

Edward roared, "Will you two listen to me?"

William's brow rose, but he'd learned his lesson. "Have your say, then, Edward."

"When I came here—and you both know what I mean now—the only way I could possibly get the castle back was to marry into the new family in residence. Their daughter's fiancé had been killed in the war and, what with her being in the family way, they welcomed me with open arms."

Livvy groaned. "Back to the archives. You wouldn't happen to know my biological grandfather's name, would you?"

"You're missing the point, Livvy girl. There's no blood relation between you and William."

"I never thought there was."

"But *he* did."

William could scarcely believe what he was hearing. "None?"

"Nope."

"You're absolutely certain?" He hoped he wasn't smacking his lips in anticipation.

Edward nodded, and William ate up the ground between Livvy and him in two strides.

"What are you doing?" Her voice cracked into a squeak as she tilted her head back to peer up at him.

"I'm a man of honor, Livvy."

"Uh-huh." She glanced over her shoulder, obviously looking for a way around her grandfather, as she stepped around him and kept going.

William followed, allowing no more than a span between them. "I searched for a husband for you because 'twas the honorable thing to do when you refused me."

"I never—"

"Silence!"

"But, William, really I—"

"You test my patience mightily, m'lady."

'Twas an easy matter to engulf her in his arms, to brush his fingers lightly across her cheek and run them through her hair. Tentatively as he half expected her to bite him for his trouble, he tilted his head and covered her lips with his own.

But she didn't bite him. Instead she nibbled him with warm, soft lips, then met him with a kiss, which spoke of the fire and passion that he'd sensed in her, that promised him anything he desired.

And he desired her. Right then, right there.

Unfortunately he'd betrothed her to whichever unwed knight was tournament champion at the end of the day. The knights had laughed when he'd made the announcement, but he'd caught them glancing her way, assessing her womanly attributes as men will do.

"I suspect," he said as he let her take a breath, "I'd better announce that the champion may no longer claim you as his rightful prize."

Her eyes contracted from an unfocused swoon to pinpoints of comprehension. "I'm the *prize?*"

"Indeed, you *were.* Now you're mine."

Edward shook his head. "Oh, boy, you've got a lot to learn about today's women."

"You didn't even have the decency to handpick a groom for me?"

"Nay, Livvy. 'Tis very simple, if you'll let me explain. This way, I could be assured you would get the very best."

She sucked in the center of her lower lip, and William fancied she was tasting his kiss again. If she had difficulty, he was prepared to claim her lips again, to blaze a path across them that she'd taste until her last breath.

"I know I should have my head examined," she said, "but what if I think you're the best?"

"The *very* best," he boasted.

"Prove it."

"How, my love?"

She grinned up at him and twirled the scrunchy around her finger, waving it in front of his nose. "Why, *win* me, of course."

"IT'S THE SWORDS?" Livvy asked her grandfather as they sat in the front row of the stands and watched

William compete with the other knights on the field. "He won't just disappear out there, will he?"

He shook his head. "Nope. Just works in the study, and just with William's sword—" he jerked his thumb over his shoulder at the one still slung across his back "—and mine. I know...I tried everything else."

"So he can...*go* whenever he wants?"

"Yep."

The knights ran one elimination after another throughout the late afternoon, interspersed with breaks for the different games that made up the Feat of Arms. All in all, it was taking William all day to win her, though Livvy was certain that none of the other men had taken his offer seriously. This was, after all, nearly the twenty-first century.

"I'm scared William'll get hurt," Chelsie whined.

"Nonsense," Edward assured her. "He's in superb shape. He's been fighting real battles for six years."

"And all he's got are a few small scars," Livvy added in an attempt to comfort her daughter.

"More than the one by his eye?" Chelsie sniffled. "How do you know?"

Livvy felt her cheeks heat and her heart pound. "Why, uh..."

"And Silver isn't used to jousting. He could goof up."

"Nonsense," Edward answered while Livvy regrouped after that near disaster. "A knight by definition is a superior horseman. William will win."

Livvy nodded, as if that said it all.

"At least, he'd better."

"What do you mean, *he'd better?*"

Her grandfather was a study in incongruity. He was more animated this afternoon than ever. Stronger. Younger. Still, the liver spots on his hand, nervously stroking his jaw, attested to his true age.

"Oh, nothing."

"Grandpa..."

"Did I tell you where I've been?"

"I won't listen to a word you have to say until you explain what you meant."

He stroked his jaw again, bowed his head and scratched the back of his neck, killing time. "Well, I'm thinking...if he loses and doesn't present you to the winner...well, I'm sure they won't have him drawn and quartered or anything, but—"

"Drawn and quartered." Livvy snickered. She hoped he was teasing.

"They better not," Chelsie thundered. "I want him for my dad. In one piece."

"Whoa, now. Wait a minute," Livvy said. "Nobody said anything about him being your dad."

"But he's fighting those knights to win your hand."

Livvy rolled her eyes. Her mom was right—the child's imagination needed taming.

"Chelsie, honey, we need to have a little talk about men and sports."

WIN MY HAND INDEED.

She'd told him to "win" her, but that didn't include her hand. Or her heart.

It would be better if she just went back into the castle and ignored him. Better—but impossible.

Besides, if she did that, she'd just wander the halls, remembering that hot kiss he'd planted on her, the feel of his armor as he'd engulfed her in a mind-numbing embrace. She was having enough trouble keeping a clear head while she sat in the sun and listened to hundreds of fans roar their approval of the victors and moan their disappointment for the losers.

A few bad falls were bound to happen, and they did. Those, coupled with Chelsie's concerns and the seed of worry her grandfather had sown with his "drawn and quartered" comment, ignited new feelings inside Livvy. Feelings she didn't want to face. Feelings that scared the bejesus out of her.

"Did I tell you where I've been?" her grandfather asked again. "I met up with Buffalo Bill."

"That's nice," she murmured out of habit. Maybe she should tell William she was kidding about winning her.

"Yessiree. He let me ride in his Wild West Show. Gave me this pistol and billed me as an outlaw-turned-sheriff. I bet you didn't even know he toured over here with that show, did ya?"

"Uh-uh." Maybe she should stay where she was and not distract him.

"Met me some Injuns, too, and a pretty little squaw."

"Indians, Grandpa."

"Native Americans," Chelsie said, correcting them.

"Not back then. 'Bout 1885, near's I could tell." He pulled his new pistol from its holster. "He showed me some fancy shootin', too."

Across the field, Leo openly waved a fistful of paper money under the noses of a dozen knights on foot. Livvy couldn't hear him, of course, but it was obvious by the knights' rapt attention that cash needed no loudspeaker.

All the knights gathered on the field, half on each end.

She was sorely tempted to grab one of the six-shooters and put a hole in Leo before all hell broke loose.

"The program says it's a demonstration of a melee," Chelsie read. "What's a melee?"

"You'll see," her great-grandfather replied with glee.

The announcer took a few minutes to explain to the crowd that tournaments hadn't always been so civilized, cautioned the knights that this was only a demonstration, then gave the go-ahead for them to show just what men had done for recreation in the early Middle Ages.

Knights rushed toward each other, raising their shields for protection, brandishing swords, hatchets, poleaxes and other hand weapons, roaring their aggression as if it were for real. In general, there was a lot of grunting and ducking and banging and falling down. Only one small group got out of hand.

Three knights, egged on by Leo, ganged up on William.

Chelsie stood up on the bench for a closer look. "Hey, they're playing rough."

Two more joined them.

"They're not playing." Edward hopped to his feet beside Chelsie and gave a rousing rebel yell that astonished Livvy right off her seat. He drew his sword with a flourish. "Hot damn!"

11

"OH, NO, YOU DON'T." Livvy grabbed her grandfather by his sleeve before he could join the melee.

"But, Livvy girl, this is better'n a barroom brawl." Brandishing his sword for emphasis, he looked decades younger than gray hair and wrinkles would indicate.

Using her whole body as leverage, she still wasn't able to push him back onto the seat. She had to settle for blocking his way, fisting her hands on her hips and looking as fierce as any one of the so-called knights on the field.

"So go find a barroom. I'm putting a stop to this right now."

"Not before I run someone through."

"Grandpa!"

"Aw, just one, Livvy girl."

"No!"

"*Hmph!*" He sheathed his sword, then grinned wickedly. "Buffalo Bill promised to take me back to America with him. I guess I'd better learn how to use my fists like the rest of 'em."

Livvy threw her arms around him and hung on as if she were deadweight.

"Let go, girl."

"I need you to stay here and watch Chelsie."

"She ain't goin' nowhere."

She grabbed him by the points of his collar and got in his face. "Don't argue with me, you old goat." It occurred to her that Chelsie would be the one doing the watching. "For once in your life, sit down and be responsible."

"My brother needs me."

Livvy glanced toward the field to see how William was faring, which was pretty well considering the ten-to-one odds.

"That does it." She yanked one of her grandfather's six-shooters out of its holster, shoved him back onto the bleacher seat and stormed into the melee to save her knight.

WHEN WILLIAM HAD RIDDEN home to Marsh Castle a fortnight ago, he'd thought he'd never want to see men draw their weapons against each other again.

He hadn't remembered how much fun a tournament could be. Though this melee was merely a reenactment of how tournaments were conducted in the centuries before his birth, he had great fun showing these men just how great a knight he was. How far they had to go to be his equal.

He lunged. He parried. He thrust. All with the utmost caution and care to kill no one, until he was swamped by two handfuls of men who either didn't know the meaning of reenactment or who wanted him dead. Possibly because he'd won the tournament…and the lovely Livvy's hand.

They were an easy lot, though. Nothing compared to the knights of old. So easy that he pulled off his helm and laughed at the sheer enjoyment of holding them off.

The crack of a gunshot caught his attention, but did

nothing to stall the rest of the men on the field. It also seemed to excite the other knights who had been standing around the perimeter watching, but who now charged forward and joined in. Within moments, he was no longer sure whom he was supposed to be fighting as everyone appeared to be battling the closest man at hand.

"Stop!" Livvy yelled, then shot the gun again.

With the influx of knights onto the field, she was soon swallowed up in their midst. It appeared she either didn't know or didn't care that she was in danger of getting trampled or run through with a sword.

But William cared.

If it hadn't been for Livvy, he wouldn't have had nearly as much fun winning the tournament. She was a prize worth fighting for, in his era or hers.

He cut his way toward her, using his sword and the shield he'd taken from one of his "kills," knocking back one and all who dared block his way.

"Get off the field!" he roared at her, ducking a sword thrust on his right and tripping an opponent on his left.

It was only a matter of time before she got bumped—hard. The grass had been trampled long ago, and a puff of dust rose when she landed on her knees. She pointed the gun to the earth and fired off another shot—he *really* had to get one of those—and the knights battling around her gave her a slightly wider berth.

"Go back!" he yelled.

"Not without you."

"I'm in no need of rescue by a woman."

"Really? I suppose that's ketchup running down your neck."

He touched the warm stream he'd previously ignored and pulled away fingers slick with bright red blood. "'Tis nothing." The melee shifted, definitely moving in their direction at a fast pace. "Go!"

Her reply was drowned out by the commotion as they were surrounded and pushed together. Her hair tumbled over his breastplate and caught in the articulated joints of his armor. Its exotic scent filled his head and dulled his reason, his caution.

Grunting, he scooped her up over his shoulder with his shield arm and fought his way free.

He should have been able to dump her at Edward's feet. He should have been able to return to the melee. But, with his hand wrapped securely around her thighs, with her weight on his shoulder, her body draped across him, he no more wanted to play games with men than he wanted to leave this century without her.

"Where...where are you...going?" she asked, bouncing on his shoulder in her effort to get free.

"Silence!"

She laughed, and desire hit him harder than any opponent's lance on the jousting field.

He'd won her fair and square. He'd won his castle back fair and square, not that he'd ever admit to having lost it. It was time to reap his reward.

"William, we're out of danger now."

If he couldn't see her smile, he could definitely hear it. She was pleased to be rescued, he could tell.

"You can put me down before my head explodes."

He grinned like a jester, he was certain. He hadn't gotten the quiet woman he'd wished for a fortnight ago, but he'd certainly gotten one with enough fire and spirit to keep him warm on a cold winter's night.

"Aye, in a moment," he promised.

LIVVY HAD NO DOUBT where William was carrying her off to. His long, purposeful stride ate up the distance to the castle door.

Only when he started bounding up the stairs did she *really* understand where he had in mind.

"Thi-is i-is real-ly har-rd o-on m-my stom-mach."

His shield clattered to the stone floor, and she heard the slide of metal returning to its scabbard. Without missing a step, he had her cradled against his chest fast enough to make her head spin.

"Wow, my own roller coaster."

Her only regret was that there was a layer of metal between her and heaven. And that his neck needed bandaging before she could have her way with him.

"Did I hurt the babe?"

"I'm sure she's fine." She knocked on his breastplate. "You need a little padding here, William."

"My doublet is padded."

"I mean on the outside." She wiggled her elbow free.

She expected him to kick the bedroom door shut behind them, but he didn't. As a matter of fact, after letting her body slide down his armor until she was on her feet again, he stepped away, then drew himself back against her again. As if warring with himself.

She'd make it easy for him.

"Come into the bathroom with me. I'll wash that—" she pointed to the bloody area on the side of his neck "—for you."

"M'lady... Livvy."

The sound of her name on his lips was sweeter than she could have imagined. Full of tenderness. Full of promise. While *m'lady* made her feel respected, the gentleness with which he said her name now spoke of the tide being turned, the possibility of a future.

"Let's find out if you need stitches," she offered softly.

"You sew, too?" he asked as she took him by the hand, and he followed.

"Not people, I don't."

In the bathroom, she threw open the window for fresh air, turned on the water and pulled a fresh washcloth and towel from the wall cabinet. William studied the fixtures.

"What place is this?"

Having witnessed her grandfather fall out of nowhere right before her eyes, she could no longer question William's arrival from…elsewhere.

"The bathroom. Sit on the edge of the tub, would you?"

He did so, but she knew it was only because she pointed to the rim.

"My governess slept here when I was ill."

"In the bathroom?" She poked and prodded and finally found laces and buckles so she could get some of the armor out of her way. "Tilt your head a little that— That's good."

"I was but a child then." He sounded as if he were trying to reassure her. "And 'twas not a bathroom."

She dabbed and rinsed. "Does that hurt?"

"Nay."

She dabbed some more, until she got down to the source of the blood and found it not as bad as she'd feared. Deep enough and long enough to make the issue of stitches debatable, he never once winced or flinched. Nothing like her ex, who had always considered the first sign of blood to be testament enough to his masculinity.

She pressed the cold, wet cloth against his neck. "Hold that there while I get some butterflies. I think they'll hold. Press hard."

"What are those for?"

She followed the direction of his gaze—right to the toilet and bidet. "William..."

"Aye?"

"What have you been using since you've been here?"

"For what, Livvy?"

"For a toilet." At his blank expression, and distracted by the hunk bleeding all over her bathroom, she searched for a word he might understand. "A privy?"

"Why, the garderobe, of course."

Her laughter turned to a sad smile. If her grandfather was wrong, if a leap to another time could occur involuntarily, it would probably happen at the worst possible moment—like when she finally got William into bed.

She pressed against the back of his hand. "Keep that tight."

"'Tis nothing, Livvy. It'll stop on its own."

"Just do it."

"Aye." He stared at the toilet. "Why does that one have water standing in it?"

Rooting through the cabinet for gauze, she was close enough to reach over and flush it. Before she knew what was happening, William was on his knees in front of the bowl, watching fresh water swirl in, dripping blood on the rim.

She knelt beside him and made short work of bandaging his neck, though when her fingers brushed against his skin, they seemed to have a mind of their own.

He flushed it again, pounced on the toilet paper and threw a small piece into the water. His head moved in small circles as it swirled down.

There really was little need for her to run her fingertips up into his hair. If he had a cut up there, it would have bled down. Nor was there need to trace the hard ridge of his jaw, but it was just so damned tempting.

"Livvy?"

"Yes, William?"

He bounded to his feet. "I must go."

She slumped against the wall. "Huh?"

"Being near you clouds my thoughts. I forgot, 'tis not right for me to be here."

"But—" *She* should have kicked the door shut. And locked it. And thrown away the key. "You're not my uncle, remember?" She ticked off on her fingers. "You're not married. You're not gay. I think. No, no, I *know* you're not." She grinned as she recalled the condition he'd been in when she'd hit him with the pillow. "So what's the problem? The baby?"

His gaze warmed her slightly rounded belly. "Babes are never a problem."

A sigh of relief escaped her, right before frustration reared its head again.

"If you won't protect your reputation, then I, as a man of honor, must."

"My reputation?" She laughed. "William, thousands of people just saw you throw me over your shoulder and carry me off to the castle. What do you *think* they're thinking?"

He nodded, once in finality. "'Tis all the more reason for me to be out of your chamber. At once."

The fact that he didn't run gave her hope. He even extended his hand to help her rise, but he didn't close the gap. She did, putting her head right beneath his chin.

His chest rose and fell as he inhaled deeply. His whisper in her ear was as soft as a sigh. "What is that fragrance, Livvy?"

He could go on saying her name forever; she'd never tire of hearing it.

"I've wondered about it since you first bent over me in the study."

"Really?" She ran her hand through her hair, fluffing up her waves and letting them tumble over her ear. "Ever since then?"

"Aye."

"Coconut. Do you like it?" she asked, oh so innocently.

He stepped backward so fast, he ran smack into the wall. Not a solid thud of flesh and bone and stone, but a metallic ring.

"I thank you for tending to my wound, but 'tis not proper for me to be alone with you."

She closed the gap between them again. "That didn't stop you from being in my room at night, watching me sleep. You said so."

"Aye. But you were asleep, and no one the wiser. 'Tis wrong unless we're betrothed."

She ran her hands up his breastplate, letting her fingers take note of where they might find more laces or buckles. "Then consider yourself betrothed."

She didn't realize what had been missing until the twinkle instantly returned to his eyes.

"You're far too bold for a lady."

"This is the nineties." Her whole body tingled in anticipation. "The 1990s."

With any other man, if Livvy had found her body pressed flat against his, she'd have been appalled at her forwardness. With William, her thoughts couldn't get beyond the sensation of being close to him. Her only worry was that he'd let his "honor" win out and he'd leave her, or that he'd leap through time again.

She summoned up the courage to ask, "So what're you going to do about it?"

"Try to adjust?"

His breastplate hit the floor, and she didn't think he was talking about giving up the garderobe for a flush toilet.

She counted his scars as they were revealed. Not slowly—he didn't tease her as a stripper, but hurried out of his armor and clothing. Not six, as she'd thought, but eight.

"Do they bother you?"

She shook her head. "No. I was just wondering who bandaged them for you."

"I did. Sewed one or two myself, too."

The last thing he removed was a rawhide strip around his neck, with something silvery hanging on the end. He slipped it over her head.

"What's this?" she asked, fingering the thin charm.

"My heart."

Surprised, she smiled up at him. "You made this from aluminum foil?"

"Aye. In case I had to leave you unexpectedly, I wanted to take a reminder with me."

She started to slip it off. "Then you should keep—"

"Nay." He stilled her hand. "'Tis no longer necessary. You are engraved on my heart for all time, Livvy."

His lips on hers were warm from the sun, salty from the day's exertion. His hands roamed her body. Her top disappeared over her head with no trouble.

It took him more than a moment to figure out bra hooks, during which time her hands were free to wander, to trace the strong ridge of his jaw, the breadth of his back, the tautness of his buns and thighs. Actually everything she could reach was taut. The man was in incredible shape.

The zipper on her pants hung him up.

"Let me show you," she whispered.

He ripped them loose. "Another time, perhaps."

She laughed and stepped out of them. "Well, not with those, apparently."

Her laughter caught in her throat when his hand slid down her stomach and into the band of her panties.

His voice cracked when he fondled her intimately. "Undergarments have changed much."

"Do they bother you?" she teased.

"Nay." He sounded as if his throat were full of gravel. "I trust everything else has remained the same?"

She smiled against his lips. "I don't know. Let's find out."

"Men and women still use the bed?"

She lifted up on tiptoe and wrapped first one leg around his waist, then the other. "Sometimes." She tightened her grip.

In seconds, he had her on the mattress. By that time, with him cradled against her, she didn't care where they were. Only that they went there together. Only that he held her close, stroked her as if she was the only woman in the world, and whispered tender words in her ear.

IN THE MORNING, he was gone.

Livvy knew it before she opened her eyes. Throughout the rest of the day and most of the night, he'd been as hot as a furnace. Now, it felt cool on his side of the bed—

No, that wasn't right. They didn't have sides. They'd both used every square inch of the mattress, often occupying the same spot simultaneously. He was insatiable, always attentive, frequently funny. He'd made her feel loved and cherished.

And now he was gone. Had he traveled back through time? Involuntarily…or voluntarily?

Had she been *too* bold? He'd chuckled when he said so, so she hadn't worried. Not before. But now that he wasn't there…

No. Absolutely not. She put all such worries out of her mind.

She rolled out of bed and stretched. A quick shower later, she was ready to go find William and see why he'd chosen not to wake up beside her. See if he was as tender as she. If he glowed, as she was sure she did.

If he was still in this century.

12

WILLIAM HADN'T THE HEART to wake Livvy at dawn. His wife had needed extra sleep when she'd carried their child, and he thought 'twould be no different in this century. Since he and Livvy had kept each other up half the night making love, he was certain 'twas right and honorable to let her sleep past sunrise.

Even though he wanted to wake her again.

Comparing Livvy to his wife didn't seem insensitive. The two women were as different as five hundred years could make them. As were the two daughters, his and hers.

As were the times, in general. He had no knowledge of all that had changed—only a small portion, he was sure. Toilets and aluminum foil and guns that fired repeatedly; he suspected there was so much more. Maybe more than he could take in in one lifetime.

He mused on how that had the potential to change his position in the world. In his own century, he was a great knight, a man to be reckoned with. 'Twas a matter of pride, something of which he was never short. 'Twas the reason he walked tall and fought hard. Wasn't it what he wanted still?

Chelsie also rose early, and she joined William out on the wall walk, leaning on the stone battlement, but she remained quiet for a time as she wrote in her notebook.

He studied his land, knowing that as hard as he would have fought Edward to retain it, Livvy also would fight hard for her right to it. She needed money, and William had no idea how to go about acquiring any in this day and age.

"Lord William," Chelsie's soft voice drew him out of his thoughts. "How do you spell 'tournament' and 'jewels'?"

He gazed down at her, pencil and notebook in hand. "What are you scripting?"

"I'm writing a story about a tournament, where a really big knight takes his neighbor prisoner and holds him for ransom until the castle is saved. Let's start with 'tournament.'"

He shrugged. "I have no idea."

"Well, I know it starts with a *t*, but I can't get any further than that." She gazed up at him expectantly.

"I don't know how to spell it."

"Well, how about 'jewels'?"

He shook his head. By the saints, his knowledge here was lower than a girl child's.

She chewed the end of her pencil, then sighed. "I can finish it later, I guess. Would you read what I've got so far?"

"Read it?"

"Out loud. Mommy does it for me sometimes. I like to hear my stories. She uses different voices for different people, and it's like a bedtime story, only better."

"Is it unusual for a child your age to read?"

"Nope." She blinked and thrust the notebook in his hands. "Everybody can read."

"Everybody?" If that was true...

"Sure."

How could he tell this child he couldn't do something she could? It was downright...embarrassing.

'Twould be emasculating in front of Livvy. What good was a life without pride?

He patted Chelsie on top of her head. "Have your mother read it to you when she gets up."

"But I want—"

"Silence."

"But, William—"

"Silence!"

"It's only three pages."

"You are a most irreverent child."

She grinned. "Didn't your little girl argue with you?"

"Nay."

"My mom says I argue like a lawyer. My grandma's a lawyer, and she argues in court."

"In court? This is allowed?"

"Sure." She raised up on tiptoe, leaned on the wall beside him and looked out at the rolling hills and forests. "This was all yours, wasn't it? A long time ago."

"Aye. Over there were the peacock gardens. And a footbridge used to cross the stream...there, I think. Aye, there."

"My mom'll share it with you if she can get that note paid off."

"She didn't... How did she say it?" He thought hard, but he'd learned so many new expressions in the past fortnight. "Ah. She didn't 'nab' an investor at the tournament as she wanted."

Chelsie sighed. "I told her an' told her to sell some

of the paintings in the gallery, but she doesn't want to part with any 'history,' as she calls it. She says that's what'll attract an investor, not any 'empty shell of a castle.'"

He cocked his head. "What's that?"

"What?"

"I hear your mother calling you."

Chelsie giggled. "That is *soooo* lame."

Nonetheless, she took the hint and left him alone. In a record-breaking thirty minutes, he'd fallen from afterglow to utter, abject misery. Besides everything else he didn't know, now he was the only person in the world who couldn't read. He could think of no way to help his lady keep the castle from Leo's clutches.

Livvy loved him, he knew. But she'd fallen in love with the image of a knight as he used to be. A fortnight from now, when the novelty wore off, she'd surely begin to pity him. He couldn't live with that, didn't want to see it in her eyes. 'Twas better if he just left. Now.

He could go find the swords, roust Edward out of bed, if need be. He could return to his own time. Now that Edward was back, he could see to Livvy's welfare.

WHEN LIVVY DIDN'T FIND William in the kitchen, she grabbed a bagel to munch on and kept searching. Without a castle full of servants roaming about, how did anyone ever find anyone else?

She stumbled across her grandfather first, standing at attention in a room, all by himself, his back pressed against the wall like a man in front of a firing squad.

"Grandpa—"

"Shh!" he warned quietly.

She tiptoed to his side to see what was up. In the next room, she could hear thumping. And muttering. And cursing.

They peeked around the corner together and spied William, kicking one of her new walls with his heavy leather boots. First one foot, then the other, as if he'd worn the first one out, but wasn't done yet.

"I've never seen an unhappier man," Edward whispered as they withdrew back into the next room.

"But..." William hadn't seemed unhappy last night. Quite the opposite. "Gosh, I guess I was too forward after all."

"The man hates change like nobody's business."

"*Way* too forward."

"Go talk to him, Livvy girl."

She peered around the corner again. "I don't think now's a good—"

Her own grandfather—*the traitor!*—spread his hand on her back and pushed her toward William, who wheeled around as she stumbled into the room.

"Ed— Oh, Livvy."

She tried to look nonchalant, as if she always entered a room headfirst and arms flailing. "Uh, good morning."

Great, now she didn't know whether to throw herself into his arms and kiss him as planned, or to be demure and try to repair whatever damage had been done last night. And was it even possible to take back being forward?

Not likely. Her cheeks burned as she remembered just how forward she'd been.

She crossed the floor without hesitation—well, not much—and touched his arm. If his attention followed his gaze, it was a safe bet it was back on the wall he'd been kicking.

"William…"

"Mmm."

"I missed you when I woke up." Lame, but true.

"I've been searching for my brother." Finally he turned and looked at her. Really looked. "You'd like me to write fancy poetry and leave it on the pillow, perhaps?"

She couldn't help grinning. Who would've thought a medieval knight like William leaned toward flowery poetry? "If you insist."

He slammed his fist into the wall, leaving a hole the size of Rhode Island.

"Hmm, good thing you picked a new wall."

"Bah!" He waved his hand at the section in question. "You think this…this…*wall* will stand seven hundred years like the rest of the castle?"

She glanced at the gaping hole. "Remind me not to have boys."

He hung his head and sadly said, "Ah, Livvy, 'tis best if I go back to my own time."

She didn't move for a moment. Couldn't. And then she slumped against a sawhorse. "I was worried you might be gone this morning. I didn't know I had to worry about you *wanting* to go."

"'Tis best," he reiterated. "I don't fit here. I don't understand all these changes."

"But, William—"

"Even if I did, I don't like them. I've spent six, long years away from my home. At times I was close to death and dreamed of my castle the way it used to be. I planned on marrying again and having sons."

"Our engagement's off, huh?"

"Many sons."

"I'll take that as a yes."

"'Twould be easier if I just..." his arm circled as if it were a helicopter rotor, and he glanced upward "...go."

She wasn't going to take this lying down. No sirree. She pushed off from the sawhorse as soon as she had the logic in place to argue with him.

"Livvy, please don't look at me like that."

"Like what?"

"A kicked puppy."

Would whining work?

"'Tis best I don't stay and complicate your life. You know that."

Would honesty? "Too late. I already fell in love with you."

Never had she seen a man's face so sad.

"But I have nothing to offer," he said. "If I could secure the castle for you before I go, I would. But the method of ransom that worked in my time doesn't work in yours." Suddenly he snapped his fingers, and his face lit up. "I know! I'll hide some gold for you. In my room."

Energized by whatever he had in mind, he paced circles around her until she was dizzy.

"You've got gold?"

"Nay, Livvy—listen. Is gold valuable now?"

"Y-yes."

"'Twould pay your debts?"

"Well, yes, but—"

"Silence." His eyes took on a faraway look. "We'll need a secure hiding place where no one but you will look for five hundred years."

He couldn't be serious! "William—"

"Furniture and trunks are no good."

She stamped her foot. "No!"

"Silence, I must think. Aye, the same bed is in my room."

"Will you listen to me? I don't want your gold."

He cocked a rakish eyebrow. "I've never met a woman who didn't want gold."

"I want *you*."

"'Tis my decision, and I have made it."

She growled in frustration. If she couldn't appeal to his heart, maybe she could to his honor. "And what about your promise to find me a husband?"

"Nay, after last night, the thought of you with another man would drive me insane."

"Really?"

"Aye."

"Then if you don't stay here, I'll have a different man every week."

"Livvy…"

"No—" if she was going to lie, she might as well do it big time "—every night."

The jerk had the nerve to smile and kiss her on the forehead. "I'll find a spot in my room to hide the gold. Then I'll turn this castle upside down until I find Edward and get the swords. All will be well. You'll see."

Before she could kick him in the shin, he was gone.

WILLIAM STORMED THROUGH the castle like a wind through the forest, a force with but one purpose, ready to do all that he'd planned when, suddenly, he felt lower than a cur's belly.

Pride? He snickered.

What pride was there in abandoning the woman he

loved? In running from the greatest challenge of his life? In returning to an easy life in his castle, knowing that Livvy would be alone in the present?

She'd have no man to guide and protect her—he'd seen to that when he'd won the tourney and staked his claim.

By the saints, if a child could learn to read, so could he. If they needed money, he'd don his armor and join the other knights who rented themselves out—but only until he came up with a better solution. After all, he wasn't a man without wits. If she needed protection, he'd lop off the hand of any man who touched her.

He'd find Edward, all right, but only to bid him good health in whatever era he traveled to next.

ONE THING ABOUT ANGER and frustration, they provided great energy for getting the castle clutter picked up. Livvy had let things slide while they'd all been getting ready for the tournament. She couldn't find William or her grandfather, and she was worried, scared half to death that one or both of them would disappear before she could talk any sense into them.

And so she picked up, cleaned up, organized anything that wasn't nailed down. She made several phone calls to follow up with prospective investors, with no luck except for one "He'll have to call you back."

She practically leapt on the phone when it rang, hoping "he" had great news.

"Livvy?"

"Oh, hi, Mom."

"Nice to hear you, too."

"Sorry, I thought you were someone else."

"A man?"

She snickered. "No, Mom." *Her* man didn't even know how to use a phone.

"Oh. Well, then, I'm calling because Chelsie phoned me earlier with another one of her outlandish stories. Something about knights and tournaments and—oh!—time travel! Honestly, Livvy, you have to handle her with a firm hand."

"Chelsie's fine, Mom."

"She's getting that time travel thing from your grandfather, you know. Mom left Dad because she said he was so obsessed with it. Said he always insisted that someday he was going to go back in time and be a cowboy." Indignant laughter flowed through thousands of miles of line. "Can you imagine?"

"As a matter of fact—"

"How on earth are you going to handle two children without a husband to help you?"

"Grandpa's here." *I hope.*

"Livvy, you haven't been listening. *He's* the problem."

"Mom—"

"You should pack up right now—"

"Mom!"

There was a moment of silence, as if her mother couldn't believe she'd been hollered at.

Livvy took full advantage. "Tell you what, Mom. How about if I marry the very next knight that comes through my door?"

"Well…"

"Oops, someone's knocking. That may be him now. Gotta run, Mom. Talk to you next week."

What Livvy didn't add was that she wasn't too

picky just then about whether she married William in her century...or his.

WILLIAM LONGED for the old days, when he'd tell a footman to carry a message to Edward, another to Livvy, and 'twould be done. 'Twas on his third trip to check out the study that he found Livvy there, talking into that same black object that he'd seen Chelsie use.

He'd have serious considerations for their sanity, if not for the fact that he'd heard a voice come out of an even smaller black box on his first night.

He stepped across the threshold. "Livvy."

"Wha—?" Her hand landed over her heart. "Oh, William, it's you. Thank heavens you're still here."

He thought about last night, about how his hand had lingered where hers rested now, and more than once. How he'd felt her heart beat against his palm. How he'd waited to get kicked in the belly by her babe's feet, but she'd said 'twas too soon.

"How does that work?"

"What?"

He pointed toward the desk. "That thing you talk to."

"The thing... Oh, the phone?"

"Aye."

"Sound waves?"

"Why do you talk to it?"

"I'm not really. I'm talking to someone else on the other end."

"Who do you talk to?"

"Anyone I want."

Hope lit in his eyes. "We can talk to Edward in another time?"

"No."

Edward, carrying two swords, barged through the doorway, shoving William into the room in front of him. "I've been looking for you."

"Not to fight, I trust."

"Nope." He clinked the swords together. "Now, I'm doing this for your own good. Yours and Livvy's."

"I doubt that," she muttered.

He ignored her. "You have a choice to make, William. You can stay here, in Livvy's time, or go back where we came from."

"But, Edward, I've already decided. I was just going to tell Li—"

"Me, I'm meetin' up with Buffalo Bill again. Goin' to America."

He clicked the swords together again.

"Or I guess you can go to anytime you can think of." He laughed. "Hell, I don't know all the ins and outs of this. But common sense says you have to choose so there'll never be any doubt in your heart."

He clicked them together a third time, then quickly began to fade. With a toss, both swords landed at William's feet, steel on stone ringing throughout the room, sunlight glittering on the jewels encrusted in William's.

He jumped backward—toward the door—as if burned. Then, with an apprehensive glance in her direction, as if she might be the one sucked away, he hastened to her side.

"Bye, William. Bye, Livvy, girl. I'll send you a sign that I made it."

"Grandpa!"

"I love you both. Chelsie, too."

Livvy was sure she stood there with her mouth hanging open. William, one hand out to warn her against moving, slowly inched toward the spot where her grandfather had been.

"Cool!" Chelsie said in awe from the doorway. "He really *can* do it."

William tested the floor with one foot as he continued to move forward. He looked ready to take flight if the stone beneath him gave way, or started to dematerialize, or whatever a bona fide time traveler would call it. Maybe the swords stayed active for a while or something.

She'd worried about him leaving since she'd woken up alone. Isn't this just what he'd said he wanted? The opportunity to pursue some utter nonsense, like leaving gold hidden in a bed for her to find five hundred years later.

"Hey, William, you got your sword back." Chelsie skipped forward. "And Grandpa's, too." She bent down and reached for William's.

Livvy's heart reached her throat about the same time she grabbed her daughter, who already had one hand on the sword. "Chelsie—"

"No!" William roared.

13

'TWASN'T THAT WILLIAM was worried they'd disappear with the swords and leave him there. 'Twas that, up until now, it had all been theory. Now, when he saw himself without Livvy, the picture was even more vivid. More painful, if that were possible.

If they started to fade, he'd grab hold of them. In the meantime, he retrieved Edward's sword in case they all three needed it to get back.

But nothing out of the ordinary—thank the saints—happened.

"Oh, Chelsie," Livvy said on a huge sigh.

He could feel her relief, and knew 'twas stronger for her own child than for herself. He'd had that once. He knew what 'twas like to lose someone. How he'd gone so mad with grief that he'd ridden away from his home for six years and never cared once if he died.

Now, he cared. More than life itself.

"Livvy." He dropped onto his knee in front of her. Gently he took the sword from Chelsie and set it aside—nowhere near Edward's. "My love, would you do me the honor of wedding me?"

Her brows arched—not the response he'd expected. After all, she'd already told him to consider himself engaged once—and she'd been quite sassy about it, too.

"Marry you?"

"Aye."

"Hmm."

"Now would be a good time to throw yourself in my arms and say 'aye.'"

Chelsie was tugging on her arm, but, except for a motherly pat, Livvy appeared not to notice.

"*Throw* myself?"

"Aye, I know you know how. 'Twas a terrific leap you made off the bed last—"

His words were drowned out as she took to coughing.

"Something in your throat?" he asked.

"Uh, yeah."

"My answer, perhaps?"

"I don't think so."

He rose to his feet in front of her. "Well, no matter. I am the lord, and I have decided that we will wed immediately."

When Livvy's hands fisted on her hips and Chelsie clapped her hands over her face, he knew he'd erred.

With a huge sigh, he went back down on his knee. "That is, Livvy, if 'tis acceptable to you."

"I'm not dressed for it."

William clapped his hands over Chelsie's ears and growled, "I don't care if you go naked. 'Twill make the honeymoon start sooner."

She took a deep breath, appeared to think something through. "No, that won't work."

He jumped to his feet. "You refuse me?"

"I didn't say that."

"Speak English, woman."

Her eyes narrowed. "If I go back with you, are you going to talk to me like that all the time?"

"Go back with me? Ah, yes, I was interrupted before I—"

"Chelsie and I aren't dressed for the fifteenth century. If you give me time, I can call the reenactors and see if I can get some clothes from them. Oh, William, are you sure we can all three go to the same time?"

"Livvy, I'm not going back."

"Maybe if we handcuff ourselves together—"

"Silence!"

Her eyebrows arched delightfully. He could stand to see that for the next...

"How long *do* men live in the twentieth century?" he asked.

"You're staying?" she whispered, as if afraid that, by asking the question aloud, she would jinx them.

"Aye."

"What made you change your mind?"

He threw his hands up in frustration. "In my time, you'd lose your head by nightfall."

Her hand flew to her throat. "You mean..."

"Aye. Guillotine."

"You wouldn't!"

"Nay, *I* wouldn't. But we'd go back to see my father still alive, and *he* would."

"You realize, of course, that we won't be able to stay in the castle unless we get a ton of money by tomorrow."

"Aye." He retrieved his sword, held it horizontal and offered it to her, hilt first. "Are jewels still worth a king's ransom?"

She touched it tentatively. "Those are real?"

"Aye."

"But, if we sell it, you'll lose any chance of ever leaving."

"'Tis my choice and, if you accept me, I gladly make it. If 'tis not enough, while I was searching for you, I found my mother's gold goblets in a forgotten pantry. One you...*missed,* I believe. Together, they are all quite valuable, I'm certain."

She cocked her head to one side, and he knew he was in for negotiation. Without her grandfather there to barter for her, he supposed he had to let her speak for herself. It seemed to be the way.

"No bossing me around?"

He nodded. "We'll be equal."

"No arranged marriages for our children?"

"But— Aye. Our daughters will be free to choose."

"Sons, too."

He grinned. "I thought you weren't having any."

Her smile was crooked, and begged to be kissed. "I'll tear down the drywall and put in stone. Besides, I'm not choosy."

He nodded. "We'll fill the bedrooms with children. They may all choose. 'Tis done." He rose.

"Not so fast."

He sighed, but held his tongue. Something he thought he was in for a lifetime of. Ah, how he looked forward to staying on his toes with Livvy.

He changed his mind. "My turn, m'lady."

"Really?" she asked sassily. "Okay. Go ahead."

"You'll teach me how to read."

"You don't know how—?"

"Silence! Just agree."

She nodded.

"You'll obey me in matters of great importance."

"In your dreams."

He sighed, not in frustration, but in comfort, knowing life would never be boring. "I thought 'twas worth a try."

"Uh-huh."

"You'll quit making changes in my castle."

"But, William—" she pouted prettily, and he forgave her ahead of time "—it'll make a great bed-and-breakfast."

It was clear he was inept at the art of twentieth-century negotiation, but 'twas a sure bet he'd be better at running an inn than she would be at learning to be subservient.

"Enough haggling. Answer the question. Will you do me the honor?"

She paused.

"Mo-om."

Livvy's fingers covered Chelsie's lips. "The honor, m'lord, will be mine."

LIVVY HAD IT ALL PLANNED. Her wedding, that is. Not how William would handle it.

She'd picked out a simple, above-the-knee, ivory dress, cut roomy enough in the waist to be comfortable all day. It was flattering, if she did say so herself.

She ditched the ponytail and scrunchy in favor of a spectacular French braid, and tucked in baby's breath for the crowning touch.

Chelsie, in a smaller version of Livvy's dress, was going to give her away in Marsh Castle's family chapel. She'd practiced diligently, even though she could do it with her eyes closed.

Those were the plans, anyway. She knew William was throwing in his two cents when she answered a

knock at her bedroom door and opened it to find a
huge white box, tied with a large silver bow, adorned
with a hundred or so tinfoil hearts, resting at her feet.

In tidy, printed letters, a note said, "To Livvy,
Love William."

That he had to have learned from Chelsie in the
past week, because she knew a couple of those words
hadn't come up along with "bee" and "cat."

"William?" No answer. "Chelsie!" Still no answer.

What was a bride to do? She opened the lid.

"Oh, my."

It was ivory, too, elegant and lacy and—she pulled
the dress out of the box—long. So long in back that
it had to be considered a train.

Nobody had to twist her arm behind her back; she
had it on in sixty seconds flat. She would have stared
at herself in the mirror for, oh, an hour, but there was
another knock at the door.

"Good day, ma'am."

It was a maid. She knew that, not because she'd
ever had one before, but by the woman's uniform.
And she curtsied.

"M'lord waits for you at the front door to take you
to the church."

For a man who didn't like change, he was reform-
ing rather quickly.

Livvy rushed downstairs to the great hall and out
the front door. There on Silver, who had been
scrubbed to a snowy white sheen, sat her knight in
shining armor, sans helmet.

"William," she said on a sigh.

"Your ride awaits, m'lady."

She looked for a carriage. He patted his lap. She looked at her dress.

"Oh, what the heck. How do you suggest I get up there?"

He dropped his stirrups and scooted back behind the cantle. Silver rolled his eyes a bit, but settled under William's firm hand.

Livvy tucked her foot into the near stirrup. "I hear we're going to a church?" She barely had to do a thing to help as he scooped her up and settled her crosswise on the saddle in front of him. The arm around her middle was as firm as a band of steel, as gentle as William always was with her.

"Aye, in the village. The chapel's not large enough to hold everyone."

She twisted her head around to see him better. "I know all of half a dozen people."

"'Tis not so, Livvy. There's George, for starters. And Sarah."

"That's two."

"The workmen."

"I hardly know them."

"They wanted to come."

"That's what? Twenty?"

"Aye. Then there are the people from the village who manned the booths at the tournament."

"Really?"

"Tom, and the knights who took part in the Leopold wedding."

No sooner had they exited the castle gate and crossed the drawbridge than all said knights fell in behind them.

"I feel like Guinevere."

"You shall not act like her."

She leaned her head against his cheek. "No, never."

"Good."

"Uh, William, you didn't summon some extra knights from, you know, back *then*, did you?" There had to be ten times as many as she'd hired.

"No. They remembered how bravely you fought in the melee, and they wanted to come, too. Their families wait in the church, along with our new staff."

"Yes, I wanted to talk to you about the maid—"

"She is only one of many."

"Many?" She was feeling downright giddy. "Really?"

"Aye. No wife of mine can run a castle without a full staff."

"You found more of your mother's gold?" she whispered.

He grinned. "Aye, enough to last us a lifetime. I was able to sell Edward's sword instead of mine."

"Sentimental reasons?"

"Aye. I once hacked off—"

"Never mind!"

His crooked grin was sexy, unrepentant. "Wave to the people, Livvy."

She tore her gaze from him and looked around to find the road lined with people. They weren't dressed in medieval costume as they had been the last time. They weren't paid to be there—

"You didn't pay them—"

"Nay, they wanted to come. I'd say 'tis their duty to their lord, but I think they don't know this."

As his chuckle rumbled against her ribs, she laughed. "I think you're right."

She got the full treatment that Leo's daughter had

gotten. And more. Trumpets. Banners. The clink of William's shiny armor every time he raised his arm to wave. The prancing steed beneath her. Scores of knights following.

And William's fingers in her hair.

She slapped at his hand. "Not yet."

He tugged out the end of her French braid.

"Uh, we're on a horse in front of hundreds of people."

"I want my bride to wear her hair loose."

He handed her the reins, and who was she to argue when he dived in with both hands, inadvertently massaging her skull as he unwove an hour of work.

"'Tis better now."

It would be better when they were alone and he didn't have to stop.

Chelsie met her at the top of the steps. She held a basket of flower petals and announced, "Change of plans, Mom."

"You're not giving me away?"

A familiar voice behind her replied, "I am, dear."

"Mom! You made it."

"Are you kidding?" A little bit older version of Livvy, with a little gray hair mixed in the blond, hugged Livvy and let her gaze wander over William's armor. "If I'd known they bred them like that over here, I'd've taken the Concorde."

William bowed to her mother, and the woman nearly swooned before he deserted them for his place at the other end of the aisle.

Chelsie did the honors with the rose petals.

An organist filled the church with music she couldn't name, but would never forget.

And, in front of a church filled to the rafters with people, Livvy promised to love, honor and cherish Lord William Marsh. As he did her.

The word obey never came up.

Epilogue

Marsh Castle, one year later

LIVVY PEEKED AROUND the corner, intentionally showing up late for the family portrait so she could watch William read a story to the baby, in one arm, and Chelsie, leaning on his shoulder. The fact that he was in his armor didn't seem to affect anyone's comfort.

Behind them, on the wall, hung the portrait of Edward and his doeskin-clad wife. When Livvy had retrieved the rolled-up canvas from the desk drawer to have it hung, she'd also found the sign he'd promised—this time the beaded necklace had been tucked inside.

"Do you think I'll get a prince someday?" Chelsie asked.

"I'll find you one," William said. "If you get that necklace out of your mouth."

She opened her mouth and let the string of beads fall in place against the bodice of her dress. "Promise?"

"I don't know." He frowned in mock severity. "What'll it cost me?"

Chelsie giggled. "Nothing."

"Will your mother be here soon? Little Edward needs changing."

"You change him."

"It's her turn."

"So?"

"If she takes too long, my armor'll get rusty."

Livvy, wearing her tinfoil heart charm, chuckled and stepped into the room to put William out of his misery. "When you find Chelsie a prince, make him from this century, okay?"

"Aye, my love." His grin was as hot for her as the day he'd found out they weren't related. "'Twould be best."

She didn't know about *that*. She wouldn't trade in her antique model for any other.

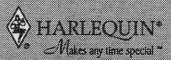

Take 2 bestselling love stories FREE

Plus get a FREE surprise gift!

Special Limited-Time Offer

Mail to Harlequin Reader Service®

3010 Walden Avenue
P.O. Box 1867
Buffalo, N.Y. 14240-1867

YES! Please send me 2 free Harlequin Love & Laughter™ novels and my free surprise gift. Then send me 4 brand-new novels every other month, which I will receive months before they appear in bookstores. Bill me at the low price of $2.90 each plus 25¢ delivery per book and applicable sales tax if any*. That's the complete price, and a saving of over 10% off the cover prices—quite a bargain! I understand that accepting the books and gift places me under no obligation ever to buy any books. I can always return a shipment and cancel at any time. Even if I never buy another book from Harlequin, the 2 free books and the surprise gift are mine to keep forever.

102 HEN CH7N

Name	(PLEASE PRINT)
Address	Apt. No.
City	State	Zip

This offer is limited to one order per household and not valid to present Love & Laughter™ subscribers. *Terms and prices are subject to change without notice. Sales tax applicable in N.Y.

ULL-98

©1996 Harlequin Enterprises Limited

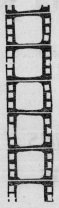

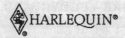

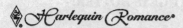

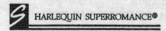

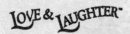